# SECOND CHANCE MAGIC

## A PARANORMAL WOMEN'S FICTION ROMANCE
## NOVEL

MICHELLE M. PILLOW

MICHELLEPILLOW.COM

# ABOUT THE BOOK

*Secrets broke her heart... and have now come back from the grave to haunt her.*

So far, Lorna Addams' forties are not what she expected. After a very public embarrassment, she finds it difficult to trust her judgment when it comes to new friendships and dating. She might be willing to give love a second chance when she meets the attractive William Warrick, if only she could come to terms with what her husband did to her and leave it in the past.

How is a humiliated empty nest widow supposed to move on with her life? It's not like she can develop a sixth sense, séance her ex back, force him to tell her why and give her closure. Or can she?

**Book contains:** three very strong women in their forties who aren't letting themselves be defined by middle age, paranormal phenomenon (psychics, ghosts, magic, etc), romance with sexy times (moderate, not OMG I have to read through my fingers), mildly strong language, and all the fear and excitement of taking a second chance at life. These ladies are doing midlife right!

ORDER OF MAGIC SERIES

Second Chance Magic
Third Time's A Charm
The Fourth Power
The Fifth Sense
The Sixth Spell

Visit MichellePillow.com for details!

*To the Pillow Fighter Fan club on Facebook for voting for which cake the ladies will enjoy, and some of the character names. Thank you for playing along with me in the group.*

*To my fellow Fab 13 PWF authors. A group of strong women and fantastically talented authors. It has been a pleasure working on this project with all of you.*

*The Fab 13 include: Michelle M. Pillow, Mandy M. Roth, Shannon Mayer, K.F. Breene, Denise Grover Swank, Jana DeLeon, Elizabeth Hunter, Darynda Jones, Kristen Painter, Robyn Peterman, Deanna Chase, Eve Langlais, and Christine Gael*

Being an author in my 40s, I am thrilled to be a part of this Paranormal Women's Fiction #PWF project. Older women kick ass. We know things. We've been there. We are worthy of our own literature category. We also have our own set of issues that we face—empty nests, widows, divorces, menopause, health concerns, etc—and these issues deserve to be addressed and embraced in fiction.

Growing older is a real part of life. Women friendships matter. Women matter. Our thoughts and feelings matter.

If you love this project as much as I do, be sure to spread the word to all your reader friends and let the vendors where you buy your books know you want to see a special category listing on their sites for 40+ heroines in Paranormal Women's Fiction and Romance.

Happy Reading!
Michelle M. Pillow

of delicious secrets! What's not a secret is how much you're going to love this book and this heroine. I'll take book two now!" - *Kristen Painter, USA TODAY Bestselling Author*

"Delightfully heartfelt and filled with emotion. Psychic powers, newly discovered magic, and a troublesome ex who comes back from the grave. Michelle M. Pillow delivers a wonderfully humorous start to a new paranormal women's fiction romance series." - *Robyn Peterman, NY Times and USA TODAY Bestselling Author*

# CHAPTER ONE

## NICKERSON, VERMONT

THIS IS NOT where Lorna Addams wanted to be. Tears filled her eyes and she was afraid to look down, so instead she stared at a flower arrangement. Her hand rested on top of satin and the smooth texture slid against the wood underneath.

"I'm sorry for your loss."

Lorna nodded, not seeing who spoke. She wished people would stop saying that. They meant well, but she didn't want to hear it.

At the sound of murmuring voices, she turned toward the gathering crowd. The funeral home continued to fill as people came to pay their respects to her dead husband. She only recognized about half of them but assumed the expensively dressed men and women knew Glenn from work. Her husband had a few nice suits but he wasn't—*hadn't been*—pretentious. Not like this crowd. He had liked to keep his home life away from his job. He called his family his oasis.

Why were these people even invited? If Lorna had been in charge of the arrangements and not a trustee, she would have kept the event for family and close friends only.

"I'm so sorry for your loss." Jackie, her cousin, forced a hug on her. Lorna stood still, letting it happen as she counted the seconds until she was released.

Over Jackie's shoulder, Lorna glanced toward the front row of seats where Nicholas, Jacob, and Jennifer huddled together. Though they were all technically adults, they'd always be her babies. Jennifer's dark head rested against her twin's shoulder, trembling as Jacob tried to comfort her. It broke Lorna's heart to see her strong daughter brought to such sorrow. Jacob's lips were pressed tight and he had been staring at the same spot on the floor for nearly an hour. The two had always been close. They even planned on starting at the same college in the fall.

Nicholas, the oldest, looked the most like his father, reminding Lorna of when she'd first met

Glenn. He was almost finished with his undergraduate degree in accounting. He should have been at his summer internship, not here. None of them should have been here.

Jackie finally let go as she made a bit of a scene, gasping and sobbing. Lorna wanted to remind her cousin that they weren't close. Jackie barely knew Glenn. The last time they'd seen each other had been nearly five years ago at a family reunion.

Some people appeared to glide through life—an average family, quiet dramas, envious paths. Their struggles, though real to them, seemed small compared to those of the rest of the world. Their bads were never as bad, their goods consistent. They looked to have all the answers to happiness. That was Lorna's life before this day—perfectly uneventful, no made-for-TV-drama. In fact, for long stretches, she would have admitted her life was even dull.

She'd give anything for boring right now.

Lorna finally forced her gaze to the casket. The funeral director had tried to tell her it would look like Glenn was sleeping. It didn't.

Lorna frowned. Glenn's hair had been combed all wrong. He hated when his bangs were pulled forward. It matched a large portrait of her husband displayed near Glenn's head. Lorna had never seen the picture before. In fact, she'd never seen the suit they'd put on him. It wasn't the clothes she'd dropped off for him.

Glenn had appointed a trustee he'd met through work to take care of all his funeral arrangements. Honestly, Lorna had been grateful not to have to make any of the decisions. But then, she'd assumed the trustee would make sure everything was perfect.

She leaned forward to fix Glenn's hair, brushing it back. There was nothing she could do about the portrait. It looked like it belonged on an ID badge from the consulting firm Glenn worked at.

"How did you know my husband?"

Lorna turned at the strange question. Her mind was in a fog and it was possible she'd misheard. The woman who spoke looked like she'd stepped off a movie set in her tight black dress and large-brim black hat. A veil covered her face, making it hard to see all of the details.

Lorna glanced behind her to the chairs. She now recognized less than half the crowd. This lady clearly belonged with them. Who were these people? Lorna's dress was shabbier by comparison and had come off a department store sales rack years ago. She didn't have many reasons to wear black.

Lorna stared numbly as the woman leaned over

to smooth Glenn's bangs down to match the photo. The large diamond of the lady's ring begged people to look at her hand like a shiny distraction. Lorna glanced at the plain band on her finger.

"Please, stop," Lorna tried to lift her hand, but it didn't feel as if it belonged to her body. Nothing felt real. "He hates his hair like that."

The woman pulled the veil over her head, away from her face. Her makeup was perfect, including the thick black lines around her eyes. If Lorna had put on makeup, she would have cried it off long before now.

"How exactly did you know my husband?" the woman repeated, her tone annoyed as she directed a withering glare in Lorna's direction.

What was going on here? Was this a sick joke?

Glenn had been *her* husband for twenty years. These were *their* children sitting in the front row. This tightness in her chest was a wife's grief. This day was stressful enough and it was all she could do to stay upright. Who said such a thing to a grieving widow? Now? In front of the deceased's three children?

"That's not funny," Lorna whispered, not wanting to create a scene to upset her kids.

"Omigod, you're *her*, aren't you? That's why his

funeral is in this dump of a town, and why the man handling the estate couldn't look me in the eye? Glenn just had to get one last dig at me. You have some nerve showing up here." This time the woman's voice was louder. "Leave now or I will have you thrown out."

"I don't know what your deal is, but—" Lorna instantly stopped talking when Jacob appeared next to her.

"Mom, what's wrong?" Jacob took a protective stance in front of her. Lorna wasn't sure how to answer. To the other woman, he said, "I think you need to leave."

"What's going on here? Cheryl, are you all right?" One of the tailored gentlemen appeared next to the lady.

"No, Frank," Cheryl hissed. "I need you to get Glenn's mistress out of here before I scream. I can't take much more. I swear to God I can't."

Mistress? Lorna gasped at the insult. Jacob looked at her in confusion. Lorna wasn't sure what to say to her son. How could she explain whatever this was? She didn't understand it herself.

Cheryl reached into her small clutch and pulled out a cigarette from a metal case. Frank automatically retrieved a lighter from his suit jacket and lit it for her.

"Ma'am, you can't smoke in here." Mr. Wilkens, the owner of the funeral home, stepped forward to stop her.

Cheryl blew smoke in his direction. "Shut up or I'll have you fired. Can't you see I'm grieving?"

Mr. Wilkens glanced at Lorna in question but backed away from the hostile woman.

"This is my mom, and that is *her* husband and *my* father," Jacob stated, his tone condescending enough to match the woman's. "I don't know what kind of scam you're trying to pull, lady, but it's you who needs to leave. I won't have you disrespecting my father's memory, and I sure as hell will not stand for you upsetting my mother."

"Father?" Cheryl swayed on her feet, eyeing Jacob. She waved her cigarette toward Frank who instantly took it from her fingers. He wrapped his arm around her waist to hold her upright. "Did you say *my* husband fathered..."

"He's our father. Not your husband." Jennifer appeared next to Jacob. She held her cellphone. To her twin, she said, "I'm calling the police."

Cheryl's eyes landed on Nicholas and she visibly stiffened.

"I think you should get your friend out of here, mister," Jacob said to Frank. "I don't know what kind of psychological issues she has going on, and I hope you get her help, but my parents have been happily married for twenty years."

"I've known Glenn since we were five. This is his wife, Cheryl. I think it's *you* who better go," Frank answered.

"That young man looks just like Glenn." Cheryl clutched Frank's arm as she continued to stare at Nicholas.

"We'll get this sorted, Cheryl," said Frank. "I'm sure it's not true."

Lorna saw everyone staring at them. The conversation had become loud and they were being watched like reality television. Her friends and family looked on in pity and confusion. The strangers in their suits and fancy dresses watched with disdain, some shaking their heads as if she'd done something wrong.

Under her breath, Cheryl said to Frank, "I don't care how many illegitimate bastards Glenn has, they're not getting a dime of my money."

"He's my husband," Lorna yelled. She'd had enough of this. "Mine!"

"Make them go away," Cheryl demanded just as loudly, "Get them out of here!"

"He's my..." A sharp pain erupted inside Lorna and she pressed her balled fist to her chest. At first she thought it was another wave of grief but, as she felt herself falling toward where Glenn's body lay in the casket, the world spun into blackness. She didn't try to fight it.

## CHAPTER TWO

### WARRICK THEATER, FREEWILD COVE, NORTH CAROLINA

*THREE YEARS LATER...*

Lorna watched the young ballerinas prance across the stage. This was only a rehearsal. What they lacked in talent they made up in pure enthusiasm. At six years old this is how dance should be—fun. Her only concern was whether one of the little tutu-wearing mice would bounce right off the edge.

She sat alone in the back of the theater. It was a small venue with only a hundred and four seats, and had been set up for both live performances and movies. The gold and burgundy sponge-painted walls, art deco light fixtures, and paneled ceiling had been that way since long before she'd taken over the management of the building. She'd petitioned the city for updates, but only managed to acquire a used set of spotlights. Three of the eleven were broken. Lorna was sure the council had only given her that much funding as a way of shutting up the new woman in town.

A plaque on the front of the building indicated the theater had been commissioned by local business-woman and suspected witch Julia Warrick over a hundred years ago. The colorful description of the woman sounded more legend than fact. Apparently, she was part of the Spiritualist movement and had held séances in the theater to talk to the dead. People would travel hundreds of miles to go to one of her shows. Julia's granddaughter, Heather Harrison, now owned the building and the old theater drew an entirely different kind of clientele.

Lorna didn't do this job because it would make her rich. She enjoyed the theater and the arts, but she didn't do this job for passion, either. She didn't live in a small apartment upstairs because she liked mini-malism and walking to work.

Lorna did this job because she recently turned forty-four and had reentered the workplace after an adult lifetime of raising children. Yes, she'd worked outside of the home over the years, but it wasn't like corporate ladders were in abundant supply where she'd lived in a Vermont suburb.

One of the ballerinas' mouse ears was askew. The little girl reminded Lorna of Jennifer. Her daughter had always been more tomboy than ballerina and dance lessons had not lasted long. At the time, she'd thought life was so hectic, but in truth everything had been so simple, so innocent back then.

Lorna found herself looking at her bare ring finger, rubbing the place the wedding band had been.

It had broken her heart to see her children's faces at the funeral when they'd discovered the truth. They felt as if their entire lives were a lie. She couldn't blame them for that. Nor could she be angry when they'd questioned how she didn't know sooner.

How could she not know? That was what everyone asked.

*How could you not know he was married to someone else when you married him?*

She'd asked that same question of herself many times.

*Why didn't you leave him? How could you stay?*

Marriage was forever. It was hard and took work. That was the lessons she'd grown up hearing and she had never seriously considered leaving him, even when she wasn't happy.

For twenty years she'd been married to a stranger. Every I love you, every kiss, every sweet moment had been a lie. How could a woman get past that kind of betrayal?

"If I were you, I'd resurrect him just to kick him in the balls."

Lorna glanced up in surprise, by not only the answer to her unspoken question but the fact someone talked to her. The parents usually ignored her when they came in to watch the ballerinas unless they wanted a snack from the concession stand. "Excuse me?"

The woman pinched her sunglasses between two fingers and gestured questioningly at the seat next to Lorna before sliding in uninvited. In a green A-line skirt and silk blouse, she wasn't dressed like most of the mothers who'd come to drop off for rehearsal. Her dark brown eyes matched the color of her long wavy hair, and when she smiled it showed a row of perfectly straight white teeth.

Why was this runway model talking to her anyway?

Lorna suddenly felt underdressed in a pair of jeans and a blue flannel shirt. Though she natural curves she'd managed to keep her weight under control through diet more than exercise. She tried to be inconspicuous as she smoothed back strands of her reddish-blonde hair and tucked the longer bangs behind her ears. The highlights were meant to frame her face, which was difficult when she kept pulling them back into a messy bun.

The woman's steady gaze indicated she was serious about her suggestion. "Your husband."

"I don't understand." Lorna frowned and reached to drop the wrench she held into the small toolbox by her foot. She shook the theater seat to make sure the bolt she'd tightened held firm. "I'm not married."

"I read all about it. If half of what they reported is true..." The woman let loose a low whistle and shook her head. "Did he really marry three other women besides you?"

"No." Lorna knew she should have been used to questions like this but talking about it still felt like a punch in the gut. She grabbed the tools, saying, "There were only two of us," before walking the opposite direction through the row. The toolbox bumped against one of the seats, bouncing back into her knee. She grunted as pain radiated from her kneecap and bit her lip to keep from crying out. So much for a graceful exit.

Lorna turned to go up the aisle toward the small office near the front of the theater. It would be a miracle if she weren't limping for the next three days.

She pushed through the curtains and emerged in the lobby, only to stop and rub her sore knee.

The physical pain in her leg was less than the sharpness she felt in her chest at the mention of Glenn. Anger was preferable to shame, and she had a lot to be angry about. Although she had been thinking about him, she hadn't been expecting someone else to mention him. In Vermont, she'd been used to the local gossip, but here people didn't know her. That was part of the appeal of her new home. In Freewild Cove she had been invisible.

Until today.

If this woman knew about her marriage, it was only a matter of time before the story spread.

"Hey, wait." The woman appeared through the curtains on the other side of the concession stand. "I'm sorry. My mother always told me I needed to stop speaking before I think."

"It's fine," Lorna lied. What else could she say? Standing up for herself in this situation had not gone well in the past. She'd been mocked mercilessly on radio and talk shows. Even the people who meant well couldn't understand how she was duped for twenty years. Her intelligence had been called into question. One talk show host even proposed the only reason she'd missed her husband's secret life was because she had been addicted to painkillers and alcohol.

It wasn't true. If anything Lorna drank more wine after his death, and never every day or in a way she'd consider a problem.

Lorna turned to go to her office.

"No, it's not fine." The woman hurried after her. "Please, let me try this again."

Lorna was forced to stop when the woman blocked her path.

"Hi. I'm Vivien Stone. I already know you're Lorna. I heard your story and had the strongest urge to introduce myself and I don't know why I thought..." Vivien gave her a weak smile. "I'm an asshole."

"It's fine. Really." Lorna made a move to walk past her.

"What if I promise this is the stupidest thing I'll ever do over the course of our friendship?" Vivien insisted.

Friendship? Lorna wasn't sure how to answer, so she instead tried to dismiss her. "It's nice to meet you, Vivien. I'm sorry I can't talk now. I have to get back to work. You're welcome to stay and watch the end of your kid's rehearsal."

"I don't have kids. I was looking for Heather but

she wasn't in her office. But you go. We'll talk later. In fact, you should come out with us tonight for drinks. Heather and I have a standing reservation every Friday at the Blues House Tavern when I'm in town. Just us women, music, drinking, maybe even a little hexing." Vivien held up her hand and slowly backed away. "Don't say no. Just think about it. Tonight at eight o'clock. You don't even have to talk. You can listen to me badmouth my ex-husband. He's a lawyer and not the good kind, so you know I'll have endless complaints to fill the silence."

Lorna found herself giving a bemused smile, unsure what to make of Vivien Stone. She wasn't one for getting vibes off people, but she got a good one from this woman.

Vivien pushed through the front door. She chose the only one with a digital bell and it dinged to mark her exit. She passed by the large front windows before disappearing down the sidewalk. The woman was odd, to be sure, but also strangely likable despite her rough introduction.

Excited voices came from the theater, punctuated by stampeding feet. Two dozen pink mice filtered into the lobby. Several broke away for the restroom while the majority made a line at the concession stand. Lorna's eyes went to the girl who reminded her of Jennifer. Her ears were gone and a loop of her hair had pulled out of a pigtail. She shook the nostalgia away as she went behind the counter to take their orders. Though she was the manager in title, Lorna was the only person working in the small, hometown theater so it also meant she was cashier, cleaner, and whatever else the owner needed her to be.

"I'm sorry. We only serve humans here," Lorna told the girls with a smile. They giggled, bouncing with enough energy to make anyone jealous. "I only see mice."

Several of the girls swiped their ears from their heads. Not much care was taken with the headpieces and their twenty-something dance instructors probably wouldn't be too happy about it.

"Popcorn with lots of butter!"

"Hotdog, please."

"Can I have popcorn?"

"I don't know, can you?" a friend challenged.

"*May* I have popcorn," the mouse corrected her order.

"Cotton candy!"

The orders came out in a rush, and Lorna hurried to fulfill their haphazard requests.

"Who's going to pay for all this? You?" Lorna

asked a mouse with curly brunette hair. Since arrangements for snacks had been paid for in advance, there was no actual bill.

"Not me, Mrs. Addams," the girl answered.

"How about you, little mouse?"

The redhead giggled and shook her head as she took a cotton candy. "Mice don't have money. They have cheese."

"Then that will be five pieces of cheese, please," Lorna said.

"You're really good with them." Heather's voice came from beside her. With all the commotion, Lorna hadn't seen her approach.

Not only did Heather own the building, which made her Lorna's landlord and employer, but she also owned several properties around town. Heather seemed to be in a constant state of motion, moving from task to task, to job, to task, crossing them off a list on the small notebook she kept shoved in the back pocket of her blue jeans.

To the mice, Heather said, "Good afternoon, girls. Are you ready for the show this weekend?"

Heather received an array of shouted answers.

The dance instructors called for order as they lined the girls next to the window to watch for their parents.

"Do you miss having kids that age?" Heather asked, staring at the children. Her long brown hair was pulled partially up and left to fall down her back. Though pretty, the waves looked as if they'd naturally dried. Her down to earth nature was a stark contrast to Vivien's carefully planned appearance. Lorna would not have automatically guessed the women were friends.

"In theory, for like a second," Lorna said. "Then I remember what it was like, the constant running around, pickups and drop-offs, birthday parties, school functions. I have two boys and a girl. They were always doing something and never at the same time or place. I don't miss that kind of busy. All I wanted to do back then was light candles, run a hot bath, and read while being left alone. Then again, now I can do that every evening and I hardly ever bother."

Some of the parents started to arrive and children ran out to meet them.

"How about you? Do you want kids?" Lorna asked.

Heather stiffened, pausing on her way to pick a piece of rogue popcorn off the floor. Sad brown eyes glanced up and then away. The moment was short-lived, but Lorna detected Heather's pain.

"Did I say something wrong?" she asked.

"I had a son. We lost him when he was seven." Heather picked up the popcorn piece and threw it in the trash can. Before Lorna could think of the right thing to say, she added, "It's okay. You couldn't have known. It was almost ten years ago."

A decade might have passed, but Lorna could see the woman's sorrow. Any mother could empathize with what it must have felt like—unimaginably awful. Now that Lorna knew, she saw how that might have made Heather the woman she was today —hardworking, focused, never talking about men or dating. She had a wicked sense of humor, the kind with wry, sarcastic undertones that belied a sharp mind and quick wit.

Such loss would have brought a new kind of perspective, one which no parent should ever have to gain. Heather didn't sweat the small things, didn't dwell on inconsequential problems. She took care of what needed her attention and just kept moving forward.

"I'm very sorry for your loss," Lorna said.

"Thanks." Heather nodded but didn't look like she wanted to discuss it further. She began straightening the items on the countertop.

"I can take care of that," Lorna said. "It's why you hired me."

Heather nodded and stopped what she was doing.

"Oh, I think a friend of yours was here looking for you." Lorna tried to change the subject. "Vivien Stone?"

Heather gave a small laugh. "You met Vivien? I hesitate to ask how that went."

"She was... nice," Lorna managed. She glanced at the remaining children by the door.

"Nice is one way to put it," Heather said. "What did she say to you?"

"Not a lot. She mentioned we were going to be friends." Even though Heather had shared about her son, Lorna didn't want to talk about the drama of losing her kinda-husband. Odds were Vivien would fill Heather in later if she didn't already know.

"Ever since we were girls, Viv has claimed she has psychic powers. No one ever believed her and she was teased mercilessly for it," Heather said. "Sometimes I think she might be right. She is perceptive when it comes to people. It often makes her quick to jump into a conversation the other person doesn't know they're having. She means well though."

"So you've been friends for a long time?" Lorna began counting the popcorn containers to see how many she'd given out to the girls to update the inventory.

"We have." Heather smiled to herself. "We just found each other when she moved here in middle school and clicked. She was a wild child with hardly any supervision. Her grandmother raised her. I was a Warrick. To everyone in town that meant I came from a family of witches, which we weren't. My mom liked the Warrick money, and hated the Warrick reputation. She did everything she could to counteract it. Vivien and I thought it was cool. I liked being special. In high school, we'd go into the woods or to the beach and used to try to cast spells together."

"Spells? Like magical-type spells?" Lorna lost track of her counting and had to start over.

"Yeah, magic spells. We'd go to the different campsites and build fires, make up chants, and even once tried to boil a potion recipe in one of my mother's stockpots. Mom was not impressed when she found the scorched metal in her kitchen cabinet. It was all in stupid fun."

"And your brother? William?" Lorna inquired.

William Warrick. Lorna thought about the handsome man more than she should have. He'd caught her attention as someone she'd like to get to know... before she realized his connection to her boss.

Heather didn't readily answer the question. She knelt down and leaned her head close to the floor to examine the toe kick beneath the counter.

Besides witchcraft and spellcasting, property management and construction work must have run in the Warrick blood. William worked as a contractor, building houses in a new development. He had the rugged hands-on appeal of a man who spent time outdoors doing manual labor.

It didn't matter that she found him attractive. Lorna had spoken to him several times and during each conversation she overthought every word that came out of her mouth. She doubted he thought about her at all.

"What were you asking about my brother?" Heather asked as she stood back up.

"Did he do spells with you?" Lorna realized she'd stopped partway through her stack of popcorn containers and had to start over yet again.

Six. Six were missing. She wrote the number down.

"William?" Heather laughed. "Oh, heck no. He thought we were crazy. He hates everything about that part of our family legend. William is always very logical and serious. He likes things you can see and touch."

"Vivien invited me out for drinks with you tonight," Lorna said. "I don't think I can make it. Please thank her for me, though."

"That's too bad. It's no hot bath and a book, but I think you'd have fun." Heather fussed with the candy display inside the case, lining up the boxes. "Viv has been traveling through New Zealand and Australia for the last month. So she'll want to talk about all her conquests—trails she hiked, zip-lining adventures, wild animals she petted, men she... *petted*."

Lorna felt a pang of jealousy. "I'm not looking for a relationship, but I do miss," she lowered her voice, "*petting*."

She'd been with Glenn for so long that it was hard to imagine another man in her bed. How did a woman in her mid-forties start dating again? Apps? Social media? Speed dating at bars? None of those things felt like her scene. Flirting might as well have been a foreign language in which she was not fluent.

Heather lowered her voice so no one else could hear her. "I'll invite you the next time someone throws an adult toy party. It's like buying candles, only not candles. You can purchase yourself plenty of new boyfriends. They're quiet, and they're fine when you lock them away in a drawer. They don't make a mess. They're dishwasher safe. They don't care what you look like." She gave another laugh. "They'll even swat stuff out of the high shelf if you swing them hard enough. Just as good as the real thing."

"If they can take out the trash and change the lightbulbs, I'm sold," Lorna teased.

"I suppose you could ask it several times and it would never get done. That's kind of the same thing," Heather answered with a shrug.

Lorna pressed her lips together to keep from laughing too loudly.

"You okay?" Heather nodded toward where Lorna rubbed her knee.

She hadn't realized she'd been doing it. "Yeah, it's fine. I banged it earlier with my toolbox when I was fixing that loose seat bolt."

"Speaking of fixing, that reminds me." Heather pulled out her notebook and flipped it open to her current list. She grabbed a pen and spoke along as she wrote, "Glue theater loose toe kick."

"I can do that if you want," Lorna said.

"It's fine. I have glue at home." Heather stared at

the list before crossing off a few items. "I need to check on those spotlights to see if I can't get them working before the recital. Anything else you need me to look at while I'm here?"

Lorna shook her head in denial. "Not that I can think of. The concessions order came today so as soon as the girls are gone, I'll be in the storeroom unpacking."

"Sounds good. I'll be in the theater on a ladder if you need me." Heather shoved the notepad into her pocket and made her way past the curtain into the theater. Brighter lights came on, shining through a part in the thick red material. Lorna went to follow her to ask if she needed help with the ladder but stopped as Heather lifted her hand toward an empty seat and mumbled, "Hi, Grandma. How are you today?"

Lorna dropped the curtain and returned to the lobby. The comment was strange, but no stranger than Lorna talking to herself when she was alone.

Seeing the last of the girls leaving, she went to lock the entrance door with the digital bell. It was the only one that could have been opened from the outside. The rest had security handles, which were long metal bars across the front that allowed people to leave but not reenter.

Lorna's knee ached, and she decided she should probably check the damage and wrap it before going to the storeroom. Now that she was alone, she allowed herself to limp toward the door to her apartment. The stairs were located next to the office and she peeked inside to glance at the security monitors. The soft glow showed an empty lobby in an otherwise dark room. Thank goodness the workday was almost over.

# CHAPTER THREE

LORNA LIFTED the curtain and leaned against the exposed brick of her apartment wall, careful not to flash her skimpy cami top at those below. With the way the apartment was situated over the theater's lobby, there was only room for windows along the one wall. Traffic from Main Street sounded muffled and distant even though she watched it through the window. At nine in the evening, everything on the block was closed except for a Chinese restaurant, which accounted for most of the cars. Incidentally, their crab Rangoon accounted for about five of Lorna's newly discovered pounds. They were addictingly good fried pieces of heaven.

She thought about calling in an order but wore pajama pants and had no desire to change. Plus, the giant bruise discoloring her knee indicated she should probably elevate the limb and take it easy.

The phone rang as she held it to her ear. Nicholas' phone had gone to voicemail. Jennifer had answered but was getting ready for a date and had to go. And now Jacob wasn't picking up. After several rings, she hung up the phone. The fact her kids all had lives was a good thing. They should be busy in their twenties. That didn't mean she didn't miss them.

She dropped the curtain and hobbled toward the queen-size bed where red wine waited for her on the small table she used as a nightstand. The place had come simply furnished in a farmhouse loft style. The exposed red-brick walls had remnants of a logo painted on it in faded white. Some of the letters were rubbed off but it looked like it would have read, "Warrick," after the original owner, Julia. The brick complemented the reclaimed wood of the table and dressers. An apothecary cabinet lined one of the walls near the stairs. The small drawers were more decorative than useful for storage. Some of them wouldn't open.

Aside from a bathroom, closet, and a frosted glass partition that somewhat blocked her bed from the rest of the living area, the apartment was one big open space. A kitchen with an island and barstools was next to the stairs. There was barely room for a small table beside a window in what could have been a dining area. Next came a living room configuration with a built-in bookshelf, then finally her bedroom area. Since she didn't own a television, reading and playing on her cellphone was about all the entertainment she could afford. The theater screened older movies, never new releases, but she watched them all for free.

The apartment didn't resemble her old life at all. Her home in Vermont had been floral wallpaper and shiny dark wood, vases, and pictures of gardens. All her plates and drinkware had matched and her liquor cabinet had been locked up tight.

She sat on the edge of the bed to take the weight off her knee and grabbed the wine bottle off the nightstand and poured more merlot into a stemless glass. As far as a painkiller went, the alcohol was only beginning to do the trick on her leg. The wine wasn't her favorite. It had absorbed a little too much oak from the barrel during the aging process. Glenn had always teased her about having cheap tastes.

Lorna *hated* that he was on her mind tonight. Even three years later, the grief and pain would roll up on her like a wave and she'd feel it trying to pull her under. It wasn't fair that she couldn't just mourn a husband of twenty years and work through that grief. She had betrayal and lies added on top of it. Her entire life had been a lie, and as a consequence, every family memory tainted. She couldn't even think of her children without that bitterness lining the edges. Bitterness, sadness, rage, she felt them all.

How did she not see it?

How did she not see through *him*?

Was there a hint? Some night at work that went a little too late? An unanswered disappearance? Should she have been suspicious of work travel? He always called her when he was gone to check in. Lorna had never been a suspicious or jealous partner. Frankly, with three kids she'd never had the time.

"I didn't even suspect an affair, let alone *a whole 'nother* wife," Lorna said to the empty room. Her words were a little slurred, but she didn't care. Wine splashed out of her glass down her cami top to form a red stain.

A hot tear rolled down her cheek and she rubbed it away before taking a long drink. She didn't want to cry, not anymore, not for him, not about him. She imagined all the times she could have cheated on Glenn if she had been so inclined—a guy in the waiting room at the doctor's office, a waiter at a restaurant, the tow truck driver who picked her up on the side of the highway. They had all tried to flirt with her. Sure, the tow truck driver had been in a coffee-stained dingy white t-shirt and smelled like stale chips and old sweat, but he would have had sex with her.

Did she even remember how to flirt?

Who in Freewild Cove would she even try to flirt with?

Her eyes went to the faded "Warrick" painted on the wall. William.

She had a good thing going here. Coming onto the boss' brother didn't sound like a smart move. But... that didn't mean she couldn't fantasize about his muscular chest and rough construction worker hands. Mm, and that smile and those eyes. She couldn't decide if she thought they were overly serious or seductively smoldering. Could a gaze be both?

Lorna caught her reflection in a mirror on the other side of the room. She'd highlighted her naturally brown hair with hints of reddish blonde in an effort to blend the white that began to show along the sides of her forehead. Strands had fallen free of the messy bun at her nape. She rubbed her cheek only to push up at her temple to watch her face temporarily lift into a more youthful appearance. It created a subtle change to her features. Most of the time age didn't bother her, but tonight she felt old and worn.

She crossed back to the window with her wine glass, peeking through the opening at passing headlights.

"I didn't want this town to know about you, Glenn. I wanted a place away from the gossip." Lorna dropped the curtain and frowned, feeling isolated and alone. She thought about the offer for drinks but knew the questions that would inevitably follow were best avoided when she was in this mood.

Her gaze drifted to her empty ring finger and then to the wall with the antique apothecary cabinet. In a drawer, three from the top and two from the right, she'd hid a small box. Without forethought about what she was doing, she crossed the room, setting her wine glass down on the kitchen counter. A wooden ladder on a track system had made the drawers accessible at one point. The ladder was missing, so she had to use a step stool.

Lorna climbed onto the short stool and leaned her weight on her uninjured leg as she lifted onto her toes to dig inside the drawer. It was too high to see inside. Her fingers bumped the jewelry box, but it slid out of reach. When she tried to feel her way after it, she lost her balance. She grabbed the edge of the wood drawer, trying to stop her descent.

The drawer held for a second, just long enough to shift her weight so she could catch herself on her good leg when she fell off the stool. The drawer came with her, sliding out of its hole. She caught it against her chest as she stumbled. Pain shot up her thigh at the inelegant landing.

"Oh, crap!" Lorna swore. She hopped toward the sofa, dodging the oval coffee table, and fell more than sat on the cushions. She placed the drawer next to her. Tears slipped down her cheeks and her head swam a little from the alcohol. She closed her eyes and held her head as she waited for the sensations to subside. "That was stupid."

Lorna dropped her arm, bumping the drawer. Without looking, she pulled it onto her lap and felt inside. Her finger knocked against the jewelry box.

"Maybe that Vivien woman is right. I'd love to resurrect his cheating ass just to kick him in the balls." She contemplated her sore knee, wondering how hard she could strike. She took a deep breath before opening her eyes.

For some reason, she always expected the wedding band to be tarnished, not as shiny as the day she'd taken it off. She slid the cold metal onto her left ring finger, stared at it on her hand, and then moved it to the widow's ring finger on the right side. Neither felt right. Maybe she should have sold the sad symbol for whatever couple of bucks that gold went for these days at a pawn shop. Could a person pass on the bad luck from a marriage to another bride? It didn't seem worth the risk. The only place that seemed right was away in a drawer.

She took off the wedding ring, telling herself she wasn't that person anymore.

When she dropped the jewelry box back inside, a second ring caught her attention. It wasn't hers. The ring had been stored without a box. An imprint in the dust at the bottom of the drawer indicated it had been there for some time. The dust had settled into the engraving. The antique metal setting needed polishing.

Lorna pulled it out and blew on it before slipping it onto her forefinger. A large black stone formed a perfect oval. She buffed it against her pajamas. On closer examination, the jewelry did not appear as tarnished as she'd first thought.

Lorna placed the drawer on the coffee table and rested her head on a throw pillow. She hooked her sore knee over a cushion and pulled at her pajama leg until the bruise was exposed. The discoloration had begun to take on a definitive shape. It curved around the peak of her kneecap like a moat around a castle.

The bottle of wine had accomplished its goal. Her vision blurred and the pain wasn't as bad as before. She placed her finger with the new ring against her leg to compare its dark color to her injury. Her hand tingled but she barely noticed. With a frown, she swiped her hand over the bruise and whispered, "Just go away. I don't have time to be injured and I can't afford a doctor. The theater is booked solid. Why can't everything just be as it should?"

The brush of her hand appeared to act like an eraser. Warmth radiated along her thigh and calf. One second the bruise was there, and the next it disappeared as if the injury had never happened.

She poked at it, expecting pain. Instead, her finger bounced lightly over healed flesh.

Lorna frowned and dropped her leg so that it lay flat. Disappearing bruises? Not likely. More like blurred vision. The alcohol content of the wine must have been stronger than she first thought. Her body felt heavy and her mind numb. Exhaustion snuck up on her fast. She blinked several times, unable to keep her eyes open. At least the pain was gone. Now all she wanted to do was sleep.

# CHAPTER FOUR

"Your knee looks like it's feeling better. I'm glad it wasn't anything serious."

Lorna glanced down from the stepladder at Heather and automatically handed her the bag of large popcorn buckets to restock the concession stand. "I guess rest really is the best medicine."

That and a bottle of red wine, apparently. She'd woke up dazed, confused, and sprawled on the sofa. She barely remembered going to sleep.

Lorna climbed down from the ladder to grab hot dog buns and the frozen soft pretzels she'd taken out of the freezer to thaw.

"If I didn't know better, I would think it was an excuse not to come out with us last night," Heather said. Before Lorna could respond, she quickly added, "But I know better."

"I don't think I would have made good company, honestly." Lorna gave a small sigh. "I ended up throwing myself a bit of a pity party."

Heather's expression turned into one of concern. "Did something happen?"

"I think I was just feeling old. My leg was hurting. I was alone. I started thinking of all the past nonsense in my life and..." Lorna shrugged, consciously not adding the fact none of her kids had been available to talk to her. How could she complain about that to a woman who had lost her son? At least she knew her kids were safe and healthy.

"Yeah, I've had those nights. Add a couple of cranberry vodkas and sad movies into the mix and I turn into a real self-pity-party mess," Heather admitted.

"Red wine for me last night," Lorna said. "A whole bottle. I'd never had the brand before and it must have been a strong one because I barely remember falling asleep on my couch."

Heather gave a small laugh and nodded. "We still have some time before the ballet recital tonight. Let me know if you need to rest. I can finish stocking the concessions."

"You have to be the nicest boss in the world, but honestly, I feel amazing." Lorna pushed through the storeroom door and held it open. Heather followed her. "When I woke up nothing hurt, it looked like I had sleep-cleaned my apartment, and I felt... just better."

Actually, that cleaning part had been weird. She remembered pulling out a drawer from the apothecary cabinet to look at her wedding ring, but the drawer had been returned to its home. The step stool had been righted and put away. The bottle was in the trash, her wine glass cleaned, and even her bedding smoothed.

"I must have done my laundry too," Lorna said. "Either that or cleaning elves live in the walls."

"If that's true, can I borrow a couple of them? I just found out one of my tenants has been hoarding pizza boxes stuffed with old newspapers in his basement." Heather gave a small shudder. "Evidently, they make for the perfect stacking storage and creating a home for rodents."

"What are you going to do? Evict him?"

"I have grounds, but he doesn't have family around

43

here that he can go to and is on a fixed income. I finally convinced him to let me bring in a cleaner once a week to help. She'll keep an eye on him and make sure he's eating something other than pizza." Heather sighed, looking tired. "Between us, after property taxes and whatnot, if I use what's left of his rent payments for the cleaners that place will maybe break even. I just hope none of the other tenants get wind of it and want the same service."

"That's extremely kind of you," Lorna said.

"It is what it is. He's a nice man. If I'm ever in his place, I'd want someone to do the same for me." Heather shrugged in dismissal before changing the subject. "But, hey, maybe lay off that brand of wine if you don't remember doing all those things. That's concerning."

Lorna nodded. "Agreed."

They set the supplies on the counter. Lorna began unpacking and putting them into their places. Heather grabbed a bottle of window cleaner and wiped down the front of the candy display.

Noticing the ring on her forefinger, Lorna held up her hand and said, "I found this last night upstairs. I wanted to make sure it wasn't yours."

Heather leaned over the counter to look at it and shook her head. "Not mine. It's pretty, though. Might have belonged to a past tenant. I say finders-keepers.

It suits you."

"That's good because I think it's stuck on my finger." Lorna gave it a small tug to emphasize her meaning.

"You know, that's strange. I found a ring after I got home last night. I was taking receipt boxes from the top of my office closet so I wouldn't forget to get my paperwork over to the accountant this week, and the ring fell on my head." Heather searched the pockets of her flannel shirt before digging into her jeans. She pulled out a delicate white-gold band with a small, dark stone. It had hooked onto the tip of her finger. "I planned on dropping by the jewelers to get it cleaned."

"That is a random coincidence." Lorna came around to look at the ring. "It looks pretty clean to me."

Heather held it up and hummed. "So it does. I would have sworn it was dirtier." She pushed it fully onto her forefinger and lifted her hand for inspection. "Cool. Now we're both trendy."

"Practically teenagers," Lorna said.

Heather shook her head. "Ugh, you couldn't pay me to be a teenager again—all those hormones and angst. I miss the energy, but it's like they say, youth is wasted on the young. If I could find my past self, I'd tell her maybe fewer paranormal novels and more math. You're not starting a coven, but you'll save a ton of money not hiring an accountant."

"A coven?" Lorna chuckled. "Did you and Vivien try to recruit help for your spells?"

"Why? Are you looking for a new hobby?" Heather teased.

"Maybe. Got a spell to take five pounds of fried crab Rangoon off my hiney?"

"The ones from across the street?" Heather moaned. "Those things are evil, aren't they?"

"I can't stop eating them," Lorna admitted.

"You look great. I wouldn't worry about those five pounds." Heather lifted her forefinger studying the ring. "I wish I could remember where I got this. Maybe my ex bought it for me? I'll have to ask him the next time I talk to him."

"Do the two of you get along?" Lorna asked.

"We didn't part ways because we didn't love each other." Heather took a deep breath. "I'd rather not talk about my divorce."

"Hey, I've been meaning to ask. Is what they say about your grandma true? All I know is what I've read on the plaque." Lorna had wanted to ask Heather about Julia but had never known the right time to broach the subject. "Did she really do what it says?"

"My grandma was a bit of a free spirit. She was a well-known medium and would host séances. What she could and couldn't do is up for debate. I already told you how much my mom hated it, but I was convinced witchcraft and magic flowed in my veins. I always felt different from the other girls. I wore black and cast my mystical spells. I wanted Bobby Turner to take me on a date, and when he asked me to the school dance like two months after I cast a love spell, naturally that meant I had superpowers. He dumped me the next day for Karen Smithers but that's beside the point."

"Clearly that's proof of magic." Lorna chuckled.

"Right?" Heather drawled wryly. "Anyway, if the family magic works is up for debate."

"So did Julia use those trick tables with uneven legs and secret levers for her séances?"

Heather studied the ring on her finger. It looked as if she would say more, but she hummed softly to herself and waved her hand in dismissal. "Trust me. You don't want to hear the crazy hocus-pocus of my family tree without a stiff drink in your hand."

Lorna started to answer that she did, in fact, want to hear about it when it occurred to her that she

47

might have inadvertently insulted Julia by implying she was a fraud. Before she could apologize, movement caught her attention. A white cat ran across the front of the theater.

She pointed after it. "We have a visitor."

Heather turned and gave a small laugh. The cat made a beeline for the office. "That's Ace. Someone must have let him inside. He's a harmless scamp who usually lives at the bookstore but occasionally he comes around for a visit."

Heather didn't appear concerned.

"There you are. Why aren't you picking up your phone?" William came from the direction of the side door leading to the alleyway. She'd only ever saw him in t-shirts, jeans, and work boots, so the button-down shirt instantly drew her attention. His brown hair appeared clean-cut while his shorter beard added a bit of rebellion to the look. He was the unfair combination of brooding and sexy, and he caught her eye every time she saw him.

Those meetings had undoubtedly been more memorable for Lorna than they were for him.

He wasn't anything like her late husband. Glenn had been charming and loud. When he walked into a room, he demanded notice and kept it. Maybe that's why she was fascinated by William. He did most of his talking with his green eyes and didn't seem to care about being the center of attention.

Lorna had thought she was past certain stages of her life. Being single was one of them. It felt strange to admit she was attracted to someone. But then to act on it? How did she even do that? She'd been horrible at flirting when she was twenty and pretty and fit into a size six. She'd never really dated. Glenn had pursued her.

Lorna wasn't body conscious. She'd outgrown that insecurity. It had been years since she'd been a size six, but when it came to dating society continually told her that men wanted younger, newer, prettier.

"Hey, Lorna, good to see you again," William said when she merely stared at him.

"Hey." She nodded, telling herself to smile, then reminding herself not to smile for too long.

"Did you let Ace in?" Heather asked her brother.

"He wanted to visit you," William answered with a small smirk. "He misses you."

"You're so helpful." Heather sighed, even as Lorna got the impression that she didn't mind her brother teasing her. "Why were you trying to call me?"

"I missed you, too," William said.

"Oh, no, what? Money or Mom?" Heather asked.

"It's never money." William chuckled.

"I know, but a girl can dream." Heather rubbed her temples. "What did she do?"

"Fired the gardener you hired for her. She thinks he was peeping in her windows." William lifted his hands as if he was done with the situation.

"I didn't hire a gardener for her." Heather looked more exasperated than worried. "I hired a lawn service to come by and mow. They're the same crew that does all my rental properties. They're solid."

Lorna busied herself while they spoke, staying on the sidelines of the conversation.

"They also have riding lawn mowers that seat them high enough to see into her living room window, and one of the guys was peeping at her," William said.

Heather grimaced. "Tell Mom to close her curtains and stop saying the word *peeping*."

"Peep. Peep. Peep." William laughed when she tried to swat him. "What are you going to do about it?"

"Me? Oh, no. It's your turn." Heather picked up the bottle of window cleaner off the floor by the candy case and handed it to Lorna. "Get your lawn mower ready, favorite child."

"Would you just call her? See if you can't smooth it out?" William insisted. "She'll listen to you."

"I was thinking about going down to the coffee shop. Does anyone want anything?" Lorna wanted to give them some privacy.

"Great idea, I'll walk with you." William patted his sister on the shoulder and gestured for Lorna to join him. "You can call her while we're gone."

"Heather?" Lorna asked.

"Latte," Heather muttered, still staring at William. "And maybe a new brother."

"I love you." William touched his hand over his heart.

"Yeah, me too." Heather wrinkled her nose and waved at them to leave. "Oh, can you let Melba know Ace is here so she doesn't worry? Tell her I'll leave food out for him."

"Will do," William answered.

Lorna hadn't been expecting the company. He held open the door for her and walked along the street side of the sidewalk. She wasn't sure why she noticed the etiquette, but her attention was focused on his actions. His gaze swept her face, and she forced her eyes forward.

"Are you enjoying your new town?" he asked.

"It's nice here. I've been down to the beach a few

times but haven't explored past city limits too much. I like working for your sister. She's been amazing." Lorna twisted the ring on her forefinger. "She was telling me about Julia Warrick when you came in."

She felt a subtle change in William's demeanor. "They're just stories."

"So it's not true? She wasn't a medium?" Lorna asked.

They passed a couple on the sidewalk, and William said a quick hello. He paused to let them walk away before answering, "No, Julia claimed to be but she wasn't." He took a deep breath and sighed. "Please tell me you're not into that stuff like my sister. You seem sensible. Don't let her stories of family history influence you."

"I can see why people want to believe they can communicate with the dead." Lorna had that same wish herself. What was wrong with needing answers and trying to find them?

"But wanting something and getting something are two different things," William countered. "I love my sister, but Heather always thought we had some great witch legacy. Having a con artist in the family who takes money to pretend to talk to loved ones, to me, is a family shame, not a family badge of honor. I want nothing to do with that. I even sold Heather my half of the Warrick building inheritance for a dollar. If it weren't a historical landmark, I would have torn my half down."

Obviously, this was a sensitive topic for him. Lorna didn't intend to comment further.

"I'm sorry. This is a strange turn of conversation. My family has been living with Grandma Julia's eccentricities for generations. I can't tell you how many times people have heard my last name and then asked me if I can see their dead relatives with them. Sometimes they're teasing. Sometimes they're serious and desperate. One lady tried to shove money down my shirt and began screaming when I wouldn't help her. Deluding yourself about the great beyond isn't helping anyone," William said. They turned the corner toward the coffee shop. "And I have no idea why I keep talking about this." He gave her an apologetic smile. "You were telling me how you like living in Freewild Cove."

"It's fine, nice. I'm settling in." Lorna could empathize with his frustration but found his strongly expressed opinions slightly off-putting. "That must be very difficult to have people asking those things of you."

He stopped walking several feet short of the coffee shop door. "You want to say something more, don't you? You're agitating your ring and I feel a giant *but* at the end of that sentence."

Lorna glanced down to where she twisted the ring on her finger and released it as she debated answering. "Okay. Yes. I get how it would be difficult to have people asking you if you can talk to their deceased family members, *but* it's a little harsh to call the need to believe in something a delusion. Sometimes people just need answers. Sometimes those answers can only be given by someone who is no longer with us."

"People?" he repeated.

"Yes, people."

"You mean you." William's eyes said more than his words, and he looked at her as if he knew all the secrets she was hiding. A cool breeze swept down the sidewalk and clouds moved over the sun, casting a shadow over them.

"Fine, yes, I mean me." Lorna crossed her arms over her chest, feeling exposed. All the emotions she repressed rose to the surface. She glanced to the side, seeing a couple holding coffee cups staring at her. "It's all over town, isn't it? Everyone knows about me, don't they?"

"Well, I—"

"I need to get back to work." Lorna kept her head

held high and her expression even. She walked past the bookstore window to go inside the coffee shop. The smell of coffee overwhelmed the narrow wooden room. Everything appeared to be for sale except the wi-fi. Paintings from local artists hung on the wall next to displayed t-shirts. A lady sold assorted pastries to the right as the line for coffee formed to the left. Tea tins and homemade jams crowded kiosks. A display near the cash register held hand-crafted necklaces.

"He's beautiful, isn't he?" Vivien suddenly appeared next to her.

"Excuse me?" Lorna gave a small jolt of surprise. What was with this woman? Did she always start conversations in the middle as if the other person had been listening to the thoughts inside her head?

"William. He's got that James-Dean-Gerard-Butler-bad-boy-brooding-sex-machine vibe," Vivien whispered as if she shared a girlish secret. Then louder, she said, "Hey, Janet, how are those grand-kids? And is that a new jam flavor I see?"

When the woman by the pastries answered Vivien, Lorna's gaze moved to the window to see William walk toward the bookstore to talk to Melba about her cat.

"Try this." Vivien handed a small cracker with a green gelatinous substance on it.

"What is it?" Lorna asked, sniffing it.

"Green pepper jelly," Vivien said. "Tell me if it's any good."

Lorna put it in her mouth and chewed. "Spicy-sweet. Not usually what I think when I think jelly. It would be good in a pork glaze."

"Do you cook?"

Lorna nodded. "Sometimes. When I have people to cook for."

Vivien turned and grabbed a jar. "Thanks, Janet. I'll pay with my coffee." She turned to Lorna and handed her the jelly. "Welcome to Freewild Cove. Janet said to pour it over softened cream cheese and serve it like a dip with crackers at your next party."

"Uh, thanks," Lorna said in surprise. She glanced over her shoulder. William wasn't outside. "So, can I ask, are you and William...?"

Vivien shook her head in denial. "Dating a friend's brother didn't seem advisable when I was in middle and high school. Then he just fell into the friend zone so I've never considered him in that way." She gave Lorna a strained look. "Not that I've ever dated a friend's brother to have definitive proof that it's a bad idea, so if you wanted to try—"

"I don't," Lorna interrupted.

Vivien hummed and looked as if she knew differently. "If you say so."

Lorna pretended to study the jar as she rolled it in her hands.

"I'm sorry you couldn't make it out for drinks with us. I think you would have had fun. Twenty-something tourists stopped for the night." She winked. "So pretty to look at, and so transparent. One spilled beer on his shirt and did a little material-lift-up maneuver to unnecessarily check out the mess he made just so all the ladies would get a peek at his stomach. He had great abs, by the way. Well done, college lad. That was one boy who hits the gym more than the books, I guarantee it."

"My kids are college age," Lorna said. "I don't tend to think of that age group in that way."

"Oh, yeah, I can see that," Vivien acknowledged. "I don't have kids, so I guess I don't think about it the same way you do. Don't get me wrong. When it comes to dating, I tend to draw the line at mid-twenties. I might be an eternal cougar. I think it's because the love of my life was that age when he died, and their energy reminds me of him."

To that, Lorna could relate. Four years ago she

would have said Glenn was the love of her life. She just wasn't the love of his. "I'm sorry you lost him."

"That's sweet of you. It was a long time ago." Vivien touched the corner of her eye as if to stop a tear from forming. "Oh, but he was beautiful. Seeing them left me nostalgic. I went home and pulled boxes out of the attic and ended up looking at old photos. Man, I was so young and clueless. I thought the world was ours and would last forever."

"What happened to him?" Lorna asked. The woman clearly wanted to talk about it.

"Cancer. I was twenty-two and we'd been married for four years, three amazing ones before he found out he was sick. Sam was a grade above me in high school. We were inseparable. Everyone said we were stupid for getting married so young but as soon as I turned eighteen, we eloped. We had no money, no family support, and I would give everything to have that time back. It happened so fast. One day he was laughing and trying to convince me we could live in a van and camp along the coast. The next he was in the hospital. That last year was nothing but doctors and tests and..." Vivien took a deep breath and again touched the corner of her eye. Lorna noticed a ring on her forefinger. "None of it mattered."

Vivien shook her body as if she could push off the sadness. "Anyway, enough of that. Let's talk about anything else."

The line moved forward, inching them closer to place an order. She felt someone standing a little too closely behind them. When she looked back, she half expected it to be William. A bearded man smiled. Lorna nodded once and inched away from him to regain some of her personal space.

"That's a pretty ring." Lorna gestured at Vivien's hand.

"Isn't it? I don't remember owning it, but I found it last night in my memory box." She held up her hand. "This is the only finger it fits on. I think I'm a little swollen because it doesn't want to come off."

"Last night?" Lorna looked at her own hand. "That's so weird."

"Why is that weird?"

"Because I found this ring last night." Lorna held up her hand. "And it fits snug on my finger."

"Oh, pretty," Vivien said. "It looks good on you."

"And Heather found a ring going through tax receipts or something." Lorna's hand began to tingle. "Was yours tarnished until you put it—"

"What can I get you, ladies?" Stu, the young man behind the counter, asked. His long hair pulled into a man-bun on the top of his head. Lorna knew him from when she'd come to the shop before. Barista wasn't his real *gig*, as he put it. He was a musician. His current specialty was playing for tourists down at the beach, hoping to be discovered by the right one passing through town.

"Two vanilla lattes and..." She glanced toward the window. William stood outside, waiting. He hadn't mentioned what he wanted.

"Make that three," Vivien said. "And throw in an extra shot of espresso."

"Make it four," Lorna decided. She pulled her bank card out of her back pocket, ready to swipe.

"Put it on my tab," Vivien intercepted. "And the green jelly too."

Stu nodded in understanding. "Caffeine overload coming right up."

"Thank you," Lorna said.

Vivien agitated her hand as they stepped along the counter to where they would pick up their drinks. "Maybe I need to take this thing off. It's kind of tingly. It might be too tight."

Lorna glanced down, realizing she'd been twirling her ring again. Her hand tingled too. The vibrations were light, but there.

"I don't want my finger to fall off," Vivien continued, tugging at the ring.

"Let me see." Lorna touched Vivien's hand.

A strange rush of energy shot up her arm at the contact, leaving her light-headed. The noise of the other patrons softened, and the lights dimmed. They instantly let go of each other. Everything went back to normal.

"What was that?" Vivien whispered.

"I have no idea." Lorna rubbed her arm. The sensation lingered.

"Ha!" Stu gave a short laugh and nodded toward them. "Static buildup. You should touch metal. It will neutralize the electric charge."

Lorna smoothed down her hair, feeling the strands cling to her fingers. Vivien's hair had started to lift from her shoulders. They both reached to touch the metal handrail and received a small zap from the static electricity. The tingling sensation lessened but didn't go away completely.

"You said Heather found a ring too?" Vivien didn't stand as close as before. "I think maybe the three of us need to have a conversation."

After Stu gave them a cup holder with four lattes, they met William outside. He carried the drinks and didn't say much as he walked with them to the theater.

As they neared the theater doors, he handed the lattes to Vivien. "Give us a minute, Viv."

"Sure. I'll fill Heather in on our new magic powers," Vivien said with a wink. Lorna had a feeling it was more to annoy William than anything else. She gestured toward the jelly. "I'll take that in for you."

Lorna handed the jar over.

"Do I even want to ask what she meant by magic powers?" William inquired as Vivien went inside.

"Considering the feelings you expressed about such things earlier, probably not," Lorna answered. When he didn't speak right away, she said, "We all found rings last night and they're stuck on our fingers. It's a weird coincidence, that's all."

"You all went jewelry shopping?" he asked.

"No, I was home alone drinking too much wine and found mine in the apothecary cabinet. Heather was home alone after drinking with Vivien and found hers in a receipt box. And Vivien was also by herself and found one in a memory box," Lorna said. "Spooky coincidence, right?"

"I guess?" He didn't look convinced.

Lorna decided not to bother telling him about the mystical connection she and Vivien had shared when they'd touched hands. She'd always been open to possibilities beyond what she could see with her eyes. Something abnormal was happening to them. She felt it, even if she couldn't fully explain it.

"You were right. I had heard about what happened with your husband," William said. "I didn't mean to imply wanting answers from those who are no longer with us was a negative thing. I don't know the details, and I don't expect you to tell me unless you want to, but I wanted to say I was sorry if I made you feel bad by anything I said. My difficulties with my family heritage sound minor compared to what you must have been through."

Lorna didn't sense malice in his words, but they still made her uncomfortable.

"Anyway, I want you to know no one here has been speaking poorly about you, or what happened. I think you'll find you have a lot of support if you want it." He started to reach forward as if to touch her arm and then pulled back.

Lorna nodded. "Thank you for saying that."

A knock on the glass door caused them both to turn. Vivien waved for Lorna to come inside. Lorna lifted her hand in acknowledgment and stepped toward the door.

"Wait, there's something else," William said.

This time he did touch her arm as he stopped her from leaving.

"What?"

His eyes steadily held hers and he leaned closer. The attraction she felt was unmistakable. It shot through her with a jolt of awareness. Sexual desire hadn't hit her this strong since she was a hormonal teenager.

Was he going to kiss her?

Should she try to kiss him?

*Great,* she thought, sarcastically. *My mid-life libido chooses this moment to kick in.*

Lorna forced a deep breath, trying not to be obvious about her thoughts. There wasn't going to be any kissing going on between them. They barely knew each other.

"Go out with me sometime." His voice had lowered. Or was that her imagination?

This time Lorna was speechless for an entirely different reason. After their ineloquent conversation about dead people, she wouldn't have guessed he saw her as dating material. Then again, what did she know about dating? She wouldn't be able to read the signs even if they were bluntly spelled out in blinking neon four feet tall. Yes, she thought him broodingly sexy, but for him to return the interest?

"Is that a question?" she asked.

"Only if you say yes." He smiled. The look softened his expression, making him appear almost playful.

"Um." Lorna glanced toward the theater. She began to overthink, her mind listing out all the reasons why she should say no.

This was Heather's brother.

Heather was her boss and landlord.

She would surely make an ass out of herself.

She wasn't ready to date... was she?

"Maybe?" she finished weakly.

"How about we say that's a yes, and I'll hope you don't stand me up?" He took a step back, "Thursday," and then another, "seven o'clock," and yet another, "King's Bistro. I'll be the guy waiting with flowers."

Before Lorna could answer, William turned and strolled away.

"But...?" The word was weak and he didn't hear the protest.

Vivien knocked louder than before to get her attention. Lorna reached for the door before she was close enough to touch it and stepped to the side while staring after William.

The door opened before she could push on it.

"What was that all about?" Vivien asked. "Next

time, angle yourself more toward me so I can lip read what's happening."

"William just asked me out," Lorna said. "I don't think I can go, though."

"Why the hell not?" Vivien demanded. "He's beautiful. He's sexy. He's single. He's a decent guy. He's—"

"My boss' brother," Lorna inserted.

"Oh please," Vivien dismissed. She strode toward the theater office and called, "Heather, do you care if Lorna dates your brother?"

"As long as she knows he comes with warning labels and is a pain in the backside," Heather answered, glancing up from the desk where she filled in an event booking form. Her eyes met Lorna's. "Did he finally ask you? He's been bugging me with questions about you since you two first crossed paths. I thought his gardener excuse hardly warranted a visit. My mother fires everyone. *Ev-ery-one.* I'll send the same guys back and she'll think I hired new lawn people for her."

"See, Heather doesn't care. You should go and have fun," Vivien said. "He's hot."

"Not hot." Heather shook her head and put her hands briefly over her ears. "My brother is a dork. He still has a comic book collection and thinks hanging up football jerseys counts as home decor."

"Hey, maybe Lorna's into pleather couches with the cup holders built into the arms," Vivien teased, placing her hand on her hip. "Why do you have to be so judgy?"

"Actually, I don't mind those," Lorna inserted. She saw her jar of jelly had been placed on the desk next to the coffees. "Sounds practical."

"See, they're a match made in pleather." Vivien laughed. "She likes a living room with a mini-fridge next to the sofa and a seventy-inch television."

"I don't own a television," Lorna said. "I read."

"Perfect. He'll have enough television for the both of you." Vivien continued to smile.

"I don't think William has installed a dorm fridge next to his couch yet, but the rest of it isn't too far off," Heather said. "Who knows, Lorna, maybe some of your good taste will rub off on my bachelor brother. One can only hope."

"So he's never been married?" Lorna asked.

"Don't answer," Vivien interjected.

"No. He's never been married," Heather said. "He says he won't even consider it until he finds the right one, and when he does he'll know."

"Leave them something to talk about on the date," Vivien scolded.

"I haven't said I was going," Lorna insisted.

Both women looked at her like they knew she was lying.

"Fine. I'm probably going," Lorna mumbled.

"You're both adults. I'm staying out of it. Do whatever you like, but if it's naughty I don't want to hear the details," Heather said.

"I on the other hand want all the sordid details," Vivien put forth. "And pictures if you can manage them. Video is better. Let me know if you want help picking out costumes for—"

"And with those traumatizing thoughts," Heather pushed up from the desk and tapped the stack of papers to make them even, "I'm going to go pour bleach on my brain until I forget I heard any of that." She glanced up at the clock and then the security monitor of the front lobby. "The ballerinas will be arriving soon."

"I'll start the popcorn and hotdogs." Lorna reached over to grab one of the lattes out of the holder.

"What about our ring power?" Vivien asked. "Aren't we going to tell her?"

"I should start cooking if everything is going to be

ready in time," Lorna said.

"What ring thing?" Heather asked.

Lorna held up her hand. "We all found one last night. It's a strange coincidence."

"There is power in threes," Vivien said. "Magic. Death. Julia always said to look out for multiples of three. This has to mean something. Like a sign."

"A sign?" Heather gave a small laugh.

"Okay, not a sign. More like destiny," Vivien insisted. "Inevitable. Fate."

"Inevitable?" Heather gave a slow nod but looked like she was humoring Vivien more than believing her. "Like how women our age start to get peri-menopausal. So, not only do we get hot flashes, they come with decoder rings?"

Lorna chuckled at Heather's wit. She noticed one of the dance instructors on the security monitor coming in the front door. "I'm sorry, but I need to get out there. I don't want my boss to fire me."

"I'll fill her in on what happened in the coffee shop, and tonight we'll meet here after the show," Vivien said. As Lorna left to go to work, she swore she heard the woman add, "This is just like the sort of magical event your grandma used to talk about. Is Julia still haunting the place? Can you ask her if this means we're finally real witches?"

# CHAPTER FIVE

LORNA HAD two trains of thought on the matter of Julia Warrick haunting the theater if she allowed herself to believe in the possibility. First, it was a neat idea, a kind of up-late-playing-with-the-Ouija-board-girl-party scenario. Second, it was terrifying in the sense that she slept every night alone in the old building, and now every creak and whine would set her on edge. It seemed ridiculous that a woman in her forties would suddenly become afraid of ghosts.

The ballerinas commanded an almost full house. Lorna watched the dancing mice performance from the back but found her eyes drifting to where she'd seen Heather acknowledge her grandma. No other-worldly beings were there amongst the living, at least none that she could see between the backs of heads.

Lorna felt a gentle tap on her shoulder and turned around. Her arm bumped the curtain blocking the light from the front and she pushed through. Besides a woman coming from the restrooms, the lobby was empty.

She rubbed her shoulder, realizing she must have leaned into something and mistook the feeling as a tap.

Ace's eyes met hers. It looked like he wanted someone to open the door to her apartment. Lorna made a move toward him. He waited until she was close and then turned to walk toward the office.

"I can't tell them that," Heather said. "We've been through this."

Lorna stopped, trying to see who Heather spoke to. No one answered.

"You shouldn't have done it. You should have left well enough alone," Heather insisted.

Lorna frowned. Was she talking on the phone? To her mother about the lawn people perhaps?

"Grandma, stop," Heather commanded in a harsh, quiet tone. "I can't hear you when you get like that. You know—dammit, did you just disappear? Grandma, get back here!"

A cold chill worked up Lorna's spine. She inched closer to see inside the office door. Heather stood alone with her hand on her head and her eyes closed as she sighed in exasperation.

"Heather?" Lorna asked, leaning into the door to look around. Heather gave a small gasp at the interruption and dropped her hands. "Were you talking to someone?"

"Just..." Heather glanced at the corner of the room and then back again. "Just to myself."

The office felt cold and Lorna rubbed her arms to warm them. "It's freezing in here. Do you want me to turn off the air conditioning or shut the air vents? The rest of the building feels fine."

"No, it's just a draft. It's an old building. It happens," Heather dismissed, again glancing toward the corner of the room.

Lorna followed her gaze. An eerie feeling crawled across her skin.

They weren't alone.

"I can't believe I'm going to ask this, but..." She closed her eyes and gave a small shake of her head. "Are you talking to your dead grandmother Julia?"

"I think the question you mean to ask is, 'Is my dead grandmother Julia talking to me?'," Heather corrected.

Lorna opened her eyes. "Is she?"

Heather rubbed her hand, not appearing like she wanted to answer.

Lorna felt a tingle radiating down her arm from the ring. "May I see your hand, please?"

Heather stopped rubbing her palm. Lorna reached across the desk. Heather hesitated before placing her hand in Lorna's.

A pulse of energy rushed through her, just as it had when she'd touched Vivien. Her vision dimmed. Heather stared at her, breathing hard. Her hair began to lift from static charge.

Lorna felt a tightness growing in her chest, created from emotions that she did not recognize as her own. A shell began to form around it, both insulating it and trapping it deep inside her. Such hardness should have taken years to develop, built of pain and sorrow, but instead grew in an instant. The ache reminded her of the time Jacob had gone missing, only intensified. They'd found him playing in a neighbor's shed, but that very specific kind of fear—that soul-shaking panic—was unlike any other feeling.

She might have been able to dismiss the reaction as weird the first time, but now?

Lorna pulled away. The direct sensation stopped, but the effects of Heather's pain lingered.

"If you tell me you see your dead grandmother, I'm inclined to believe you," Lorna said. Each thump of her heart reverberated through her, but it did not lessen the anguish. Nothing could diminish this kind of pain, not really. Time made it more manageable, hardened a shell around it, but it was always there, always inside. "Something is happening to us, isn't it? We're becoming connected."

"I'm fairly certain that these rings belonged to my grandmother. She wanted us to find them and put them on." Heather sat down in her chair. She tried smoothing down her hair before digging into the desk to find a hair tie.

"Why?" Lorna moved to take a seat across from the desk and leaned forward.

"She said our pain joins us. It called to her. It..." Heather glanced at the empty corner. "She says our meeting was destined."

"So you can talk to her ghost?" Lorna stared at the corner, trying to see any shift of light or color that might indicate a spirit was with them. There was nothing.

"Yes. I see her. I don't expect you to believe me. I'm aware of how crazy it sounds. I've been told my whole life it was my imagination."

"Are there others or just Julia?" Lorna didn't

know if it was her tingling hand, or her desire to want to believe such a thing were real that caused her to accept what was happening. Emotions were hardly empirical evidence, but they were real. "Can you see anyone with me?"

"Glenn isn't with you," Heather said, clearly understanding what Lorna wanted to know. She pressed her fist against the center of her chest. "I'm so sorry. What I felt from you when we touched..." She took a deep breath. "That level of betrayal while feeling so much grief. The public embarrassment. The isolation afterward. I don't know how you carry all that as gracefully as you do. A few seconds of it and I feel like I'm being pulled down into the floor. All I want is a blanket to hide under."

Lorna sat back in her seat. How could she complain about Glenn when Heather had lost a son?

"Julia says he's the source of your pain." Heather pursed her lips tightly together and cupped her hands over her ears. "Your unasked questions, that deep betrayal, it's why you were drawn to come here. You were meant to find us. That is why you moved here. It's fate."

Lorna wasn't sure her decision to move to the seaside town was destiny. The decision had been impulsive, spurred by her need to escape her situation. Heather dropped her hands from her head.

"I'm not sure I would call it fate. The truth is, I couldn't think of anywhere else I wanted to go. When my kids were around eight and ten, we drove through here on a family vacation," Lorna said. "Even though we didn't stop for longer than it took to fill up with gas, I'd always remembered this town and wanted to come back. Jennifer had too much junk food and threw up in the car. Glenn was in a bad mood and hated it here. We drove back to Vermont with the windows open. It's a hard vacation to forget."

All of those family memories were tainted now. They were followed by the thoughts whispering through her mind as if a force outside herself mocked her.

*He wasn't your husband, not really, you old fool. All of those moments were built on a lie. Every touch between the two of you was meaningless.*

"Maybe that *is* fate. You felt drawn here the first time you drove through." Heather turned to the security monitors. "I think the ballerinas are done."

"I can go out front." Lorna flipped the switch by the office door to turn on the auditorium lights for the patrons. She made a move to leave.

"No, stay," Heather said. "They'll rush the front door and the restrooms. We'll go when they've filtered out. I don't feel like making small talk with anyone tonight."

Lorna lowered herself back into her seat. She still felt like someone stood in the office with them. "You were right about your brother. William indicated he strongly doesn't believe in this kind of thing."

"No, he doesn't," Heather agreed. "He's just like my mother. I think that's why he's her favorite. Grandma Julia always embarrassed her. She married into the Warrick family and never understood what she called the family eccentricities. But I told you that earlier."

"What about your father? If he was born a Warrick, then did he see things too?"

"My father was sensitive, but I think he ignored that part of himself to keep my mother happy. If William has any of the family traits, he would never admit to it. We don't talk about our family's magic."

Lorna glanced at the empty corner, wondering if she would feel something if she put her hand through Julia's invisible body. Or would that be considered rude? Then again, how could it be rude if she couldn't see her? "Are there other ghosts? I mean, not here, but around?"

"You told her?" Vivien appeared behind Lorna. "And it looks like you've been getting an earful. Have the headaches started?"

Heather gave a small nod.

"Grandma Julia, or are there others trying to talk to you?" Vivien asked.

"Just Julia," Heather said. "She's chatty tonight. I can barely make out what she's saying she's talking too fast."

Vivien slipped a hand on Lorna's shoulder, giving a small squeeze as she passed. A tiny jolt ran down her arm at the contact but was short-lived. "The tiny dancers are finished, by the way."

"We saw." Heather gestured at the security monitor.

"They're adorable, but I don't think we have any future Swan Lakes on our hands." Vivien chuckled as she took a seat close to Lorna. "I think that Bronwyn girl might have a future as a soccer player, though. She kicks like she's mad at the world."

"I'd maybe keep that opinion to yourself," Heather instructed. "They're just children. If they want to dream about being ballerinas, let them."

"I only say what I sense," Vivien said.

Heather shared a look with Vivien, before saying, "See. I told you Viv is intuitive. She feels things."

"And I see you told her for me too." Vivien studied her fingernails.

Lorna looked back and forth between the women.

"By intuitive, she means I'm psychic," Vivien said, holding up her forefinger to show the ring. "It's how I knew we were destined to be great friends."

"Psychic?" Lorna looked to Heather, who gave a small shrug. Heather had already admitted before that Vivien thought as much. "So you see Grandma Julia too?"

"I'm more empathic. I can't hold a conversation with the dead. I'm not a medium like Heather," Vivien said. "I sense things about people—who they are, what they would be good at, if I want to know them or not, and if they're lying to me. Some of my ancestors worked for a carnival doing tarot card readings and telling fortunes, though I've never seen the future myself, so I can't tell you how effective they were at it. They call people like me clairsentient because I feel what other people are feeling and understand why they might be feeling that way. But also I'm considered claircognizant because I just sort of know things to be real or not without always being able to explain how I know. Heather could talk to the ghost and be directed to the dead body. I would just *know* where to look for the dead body. I've never been good at explaining it."

Lorna glanced at the lobby security monitors watching the dancers and their families make their way out the front door. She wasn't sure what to say to all of this. Part of her believed it because she felt the tingling in her hand and the transfer of emotions. Another part of her wanted to believe it because that would mean life wasn't dull. Yet a third part of her— the doubtful part raised by practical parents in a no-nonsense society—was highly skeptical when it came to people who claimed to be psychic.

She ignored that third part.

"You're not good at explaining because we don't tell people," Heather said. "And if we ever start, maybe don't use the dead body analogy. It's a little disturbing."

"Says the woman who sees dead people," Vivien answered. "What about you, Lorna? What's your secret?"

"I don't have a secret. Not like that." Lorna frowned. They both stared at her expectantly. "I think it's obvious to the whole world that I don't know when I'm being lied to. I can't see ghosts. Of course I have empathy, but I wouldn't say that makes me empathic, just empathetic."

Vivien leaned closer and stared at Lorna. "You have..." She gestured her hands around Lorna's face. "Something."

Lorna laughed. "Good to know I have *something*."

"Leave her be, Viv," Heather said. "She has a lot to process."

"You find things," Vivien stated in excitement, as if she'd just discovered the cure for some rare disease. "I bet you're the reason we found these rings the same day you and I finally met."

"I don't think that's a superpower," Lorna denied. Of course she was good at finding things. She'd spent a lifetime as a mother with a family who lost things.

*Mom, where's my shirt?*

*Mom, have you seen my mitt?*

*Mom, I can't find my homework. I need it for Mr. So-and-so's class!*

*Honey, do we have any mayo?*

"I think it's more of a mom power. When you're the one cleaning, and keeping track of everything, and maintaining the family schedule, it becomes part of the job to note where things are located." Lorna's gaze kept moving back to the corner. There had to be a way to tell if Julia stood in the room.

"That all may be true, but I think it's more than that." Vivien moved to check the lobby monitor. Two girls were doing pirouettes on the hard floor in front of the candy display and a blonde woman in a red coat stood near them staring up at the camera. "I think you need to practice using the skill. Once everyone is gone, we'll send you on a scavenger hunt. I'll prove it to you. You're a finder."

"What's that lady doing?" Lorna moved to get a closer look at the monitor.

"What lady? I don't see anyone." Vivien blocked her vision as she stepped out of the way. "It was probably one of the parents."

When Vivien moved the blonde was gone. Someone waved the ballerinas over to the front doors and the two girls ran outside.

Heather sighed and pushed up from her chair. She slid open the desk drawer and took out a set of keys. "Looks like that's the last of them. Let's lock up and do a sweep for stragglers."

CHAPTER SIX

"You're right. I'm magical," Lorna wryly stated as she threw a hair tie onto the lost-and-found pile she had started on the edge of the small stage. So far, she'd located a set of mouse ears, a pen, a pack of chewing gum, twenty-two cents, and an old cell phone skin that looked like it had been cracked before someone shoved it next to their seat by the wall. She'd been visualizing finding lost objects, which could hardly be considered a parlor trick considering there were always lost items in a theater.

Heather and Vivien sat in the front row watching her work. They both held soda cups from the concession, but Vivien drank wine from hers and Heather had soda and vodka.

Lorna picked up her cup and took a drink. The surprising taste of vodka in her soda overpowered her taste buds. She coughed and patted the center of her chest.

"I added a splash more to help you catch up with us," Vivien said. "You're welcome."

Heather turned to the side and flinched at the empty seats. She held up her hand as if telling someone to be quiet. "Julia says our problem is we asked too broad of a question."

"Find something that was lost?" Vivien shrugged. "Sounds specific to me."

"Lorna, try to find something of value that was hidden over fifty years ago," Heather requested.

"Valuable? Like the take from a bank robbery?" Lorna laughed.

"Yes." Vivien straightened in her chair and twirled her finger to encompass the theater. "Find that. We need a shopping spree in Italy. I want new shoes."

Lorna tilted her head to look at the woman's new designer heels. "I have a feeling you own more shoes than a department store."

"See?" Vivien tipped her cup at Lorna. "You *are* psychic."

"Or perceptive." Lorna took a deep breath and looked around. "Fine. But this is the last time."

She closed her eyes and took a deep breath, telling herself to find something valuable and old.

Like the times before, she didn't have any clue why she began walking. It wasn't like she felt a pull or some unseen force leading her. She just moved. Instead of into the rows, she turned toward the steps leading onto the stage.

"Valuable and old," she muttered. "Find something valuable and old."

Lorna stood on the stage looking out into the theater. She twisted the ring on her finger. The sensation of heat came from above. Her gaze went to the lights she'd helped acquire. They were off, but that didn't stop the feeling that they shone on her like a spotlight. Heather and Vivien watched her, cups in hand, from the first row.

A faint clapping sounded. Her new friends didn't move, and the noise couldn't have come from them.

"Do you hear that?" Lorna turned in a slow circle.

"No," Heather and Vivien said in unison.

Without being able to explain why, Lorna crossed to the back of the stage. She reached between two of the velvet curtains. Her hand bumped a small lever on a post and she pulled down. It didn't move. She pulled harder. The lever gave way with a loud metal clank. She heard gears and felt vibration beneath her feet.

Lorna looked at the stage and then up toward the ceiling, unsure of what she'd done.

"What is that?" Vivien asked.

"What did you do?" Heather ran along the front of the stage to the stairs.

"Stop moving," Vivien ordered. "Listen."

Several of the floorboards sank into the floor to create an uneven hole close to where Lorna stood. The slats had been staggered to hide the fact there was an opening. The clanking continued.

Heather and Lorna crept forward and leaned over the opening.

"What did you do?" Heather repeated, her voice soft.

"I don't know." Lorna peered into the hole. The noise stopped. Nothing happened.

"Viv, give me your phone." Heather went to the end of the stage to take the device. She turned the flashlight function on and shone it into the floor.

"I think I broke the stage," Lorna said. "I'm so sorry. I didn't mean to."

"Of course you didn't mean to do it," Heather agreed.

"What's down there?" Vivien asked.

"I have no clue. I didn't know there was useable space beneath the stage. When we tried to go in from the sides, we kept hitting brick walls." Heather lay on the floor to better see underneath.

Lorna returned to the curtains and pulled them back to see the post she'd touched. The lever she'd pulled was just one of three tiny notches in the wood.

"What does Julia say?" Vivien asked.

"She left," Heather answered. "I think I see something down here. It looks like a track of some sort."

"Do you want me to pull the next lever?" Lorna asked. "There are three of them disguised as notches in the wood."

"Do it." The click of Vivien's heels announced her presence on the stage.

"Heather?" Lorna wasn't about to break anything else. She needed this job and it would be hard to rent out the space with a hole in the stage.

"Go ahead. Everyone be careful. We don't know what's going to happen." Heather pushed back onto her knees and nodded that she was ready.

Lorna flipped the second lever. It was small and

difficult to hold on to. A tiny *clunk* sounded but nothing happened. She pushed it up and tried flipping it again. Still, nothing significant happened. "Anything?"

"No," Heather said. "Try the last one."

Lorna pulled the last lever.

The floor began to vibrate and creak. Lorna joined Heather and Vivien as they watched the hole. Heather held the light. Suddenly, something popped as if letting loose and wheels squeaked down the track, carrying a box-shaped object. It stopped halfway beneath the stage.

"It looks like an altar," Vivien observed. "See the symbols painted on the sides? Those are like the ones in Julia's pictures."

"I wondered what had happened to that thing." Heather laid on her stomach and craned her neck as she dipped her head into the hole. "You're right. I've seen this in family pictures from Grandma Julia's heyday. I just assumed it was thrown out at some point."

Lorna dropped her legs over the side.

"Hey, careful," Vivien warned.

"I want to take a look. May I borrow your phone?" Lorna held her hand out for the light.

"Hopefully I can figure out what's wrong and make the floor retract back into place."

Heather pushed up from the floor and gave it to her. Lorna dropped down and slowly knelt under the stage, careful not to bump the altar. Spiders had called the crawlspace home at one point, only to abandon their dusty webs. The stringy remains hung from the wood slats like plant roots, drifting in the stirred air amongst a series of frayed ropes, pullies, and counterweights. Metal gears fitted together to create a mechanical system. She followed the lines with the light before coming to a frayed edge, where it had snapped.

"What do you see?" Vivien asked.

"It looks like the inside of one of those old dumb-waiters," Lorna said. "I think it's meant to bring the altar down the tracks and then lift it onto the stage, and then do the reverse to store it. Some of the ropes have snapped, so I don't think we can retract the floor back into place to fix the hole."

"I'm coming down." Heather's legs dropped over the side before she too jumped down to join Lorna. She gave a small groan. "In my head I'm not old, but I'd like someone to tell that to my stiff joints. They do not want to cooperate."

The phone in her hand vibrated and Lorna glanced at the screen. "You're getting a message."

She automatically turned the phone toward Vivien. Heather took it from her.

"Had fun the other night. Give me a call, baby, and we'll do it again," Heather read aloud from the notification in a monotone voice, before ad-libbing, "love, Boy Toy number twenty-seven."

"It does not say that," Vivien dismissed with a laugh. "I never gave twenty-seven my phone number."

Lorna crawled forward to get a better look around the side of the altar.

"You are such a cougar." The light from the phone lit Heather's face.

"You should try it sometime. Might loosen up those stiff joints of yours," Vivien said.

"Or put me in traction," Heather quipped. She handed the phone back to Lorna so she could use the flashlight.

"Well, I think I may be only half-finder. I found something old," Lorna said, "but I'm not sure how valuable it is."

"Value isn't always money." Theater lights haloed Vivien and she swayed back and forth as if she contemplated joining them. Instead, she took off her heels and sat on the side of the hole with her feet dangling.

"Bank loot would have been nicer." Heather crawled next to Lorna to peek around the altar. Specks of dust drifted around them as they disrupted the area. She swatted at the strands of web tangling in her hair. "Or pirate treasure."

"Lorna, maybe you're not done finding. Is there anything else down there?" Vivien lightly swung her feet. They didn't touch the ground.

"I don't think..." She moved the light back and forth. Something caught her eyes in the darkness, but she couldn't be sure if it was anything by the way it cast a shadow. Pullies and ropes blocked her path. She gave the phone to Heather. "Hold this for me. I think I see something."

The hard floor bit into her knees and palms as she made her way parallel to the tracks. The metal rails were at an angle to use gravity to help slide the altar. Tiny bits of debris dug into her hands and she swiped them several times to dislodge the irritants. To herself, she whispered, "Please don't let there be spiders. Please don't let there be spiders."

Lorna leaned under a series of looped ropes. Something tickled the side of her neck and she jerked, swatting it away before she realized it was a frayed piece of rope.

"Careful," Heather called softly.

Lorna reached across the tracks for the shadowy object. She half expected it to be scrap wood that had been tossed aside when the stage was built. Her fingertips brushed the edge, sliding the rectangular object to prove it was loose. The light came closer, and she heard Heather moving behind her. Unable to reach, she readjusted her position to inch closer.

"Are we rich?" Vivien called.

Neither woman answered her.

Lorna glanced along the side of the altar where she hadn't been able to see before. Aside from the cobwebs and tied pieces of rope, there was nothing worth noting. She reached again, able to drag the object toward her with the tips of her fingers. The closer it came, the easier it was to pull.

"What did you find?" Vivien insisted.

"I'm not sure. A box maybe. It's wrapped in velvet." Lorna tried to backtrack her way under the ropes. The light dipped several times as Heather retraced her path, making it difficult to see.

"Here." Lorna lifted the object behind her.

Heather grabbed it before handing it up to Vivien.

Lorna attempted to turn around. Her shoulder bumped the altar, jarring it enough to send it along its original path.

Careful!" Lorna called out, unsure where Heather was in relation to it.

Heather gasped. The altar slammed forward as it came to the end of the track. Heather's feet slid upward as if Vivien dragged her out of the hole to safety. The phone light shone from where it had landed on the ground. The altar now blocked the opening.

"Are you all right?" Lorna called in worry, making her way as fast as she could toward the opening.

"She's fine," Vivien answered. "You?"

"Yeah." Lorna lifted the phone and slid it onto the stage before wedging her body between the altar and the floorboards. A slat scraped her side, but she didn't care. Vivien and Heather took hold under her arms and helped to pull her out.

Lorna collapsed on the stage and took several deep breaths. She swiped at her dirty knees, brushing off her hands at the same time.

"It's a book," Vivien said, pulling an old book out of the dirty velvet bag. The hefty tome was three inches thick with a padded leather cover. The rough edges of the pages appeared handcrafted. "It looks medieval."

Even with the protective covering, dust had managed to make its way inside the velvet. Vivien turned the material inside out and swiped at the cover's embossing.

"Some of these symbols look like our rings." Vivien lifted the book to show symbols forming a circle on the front cover. She pointed her forefinger and tapped a manicured nail against the symbol that matched her jewelry.

"Let me see it." Heather took the book and opened it.

The smell of parchment reminded Lorna of the special collections room at the library. She and Vivien sat on either side of Heather as she turned the pages. "*Warrick*," had been written on the title page in calligraphy. Decorative drawings lined the edges of the page.

"This is drawn, not printed," Lorna observed, touching the edge of the thick paper. "The handwriting is exquisite."

Heather turned a couple of the pages slowly, as if worried they would crumble.

"It must have belonged to Julia," Vivien said.

"December 5, 1928," Heather read the first line,

"William Turner, ten dollars to contact daughter Lucy. Said their goodbyes, spirit has moved on." She went to the second entry. "December 7, 1928, Mary Burke, two dollars and thirty cents to contact husband Holden. Spirit belligerent, as he was in life, told Mary he was sorry for how he treated her. Ex."

"Ex?" Vivien asked.

"Ex-husband maybe? I have no clue but it sounds like maybe she lied about what the spirit said. I don't see someone belligerent apologizing," Heather answered, before reading the next line, "December 9, 1928, Fiona O'Leary, six dollars to contact three-year-old daughter Mirabella. Not earthbound. December 10, Franklin Mercer, twenty dollars to contact law partner for missing trust papers. Successful. December 10, Jane Benoit, three dollars to contact mother, Josephine. Hateful woman. Ex. December 10, two dollars..."

Heather let her voice taper off but kept her eyes on the book as she began turning through pages faster than before.

"It's a ledger of payments and séances," Vivien said. "These must be people Julia contacted."

"What's that?" Lorna stopped Heather from turning as the format of the page changed into a list.

"1930 to 1931. Suicides: T. J. Wells, P. G. Grant,

Mr. Holcomb, J. J. Roark..." Heather frowned. "There have to be at least sixty names here."

"That was around the time of the Great Depression," Lorna said. "The stock markets crashed and people lost everything. Suicide rates went up. Soil erosion caused farms to fail and left some two million people homeless."

"History buff?" Vivien asked.

"Three kids, three middle school diorama projects and presentations on the Great Depression and the Dust Bowl," Lorna answered.

"It makes sense. The payments go down—five cents, ten cents, a dollar..." Heather ran her finger down the page. "Traded brooch, chicken, tomato, no charge..."

"How sad," Lorna whispered.

"It's a book of death," Vivien said. "It's filled with pain. Everything about it is sad."

"Life has value." Lorna took a deep breath. Vivien was right. This book represented many sad things. "It's old. I don't know how I found this. I don't know how I knew to reach for the switch to open the floor."

"I don't know *why* we found this," Vivien added. "I don't want to start a séance business. It's bad enough I can detect everyday emotions, but grief this deep in a constant dose? I'm not sure I can absorb that and keep my cheery disposition."

Heather used her arm as a bookmark and closed the pages to look at the cover. She placed her hand over the symbols. "I know I complain when people act like being in your forties is old and that once we hit midlife we're all about to fall apart, but the truth is my hips are hating me right now. Someone help me off this hard floor."

"My place?" Lorna offered. "I have a couch."

"Let's do it." Vivien stood and reached down to help Heather to her feet. As their hands touched, both women inhaled sharply. Their hair began to lift from their shoulders.

Heather pulled away first. "That's going to take some getting used to."

Heather pushed up from the stage, managing to stand on her own without help. She took a few stunted steps while still carrying the book, leaning side to side to stretch.

"What about the floor?" Lorna asked, looking into the hole.

"Leave it. We're closed tomorrow. I'll deal with it then." Heather cradled the book to her chest as she led the way down the stairs. Vivien slipped her feet into her heels and Lorna offered an arm to help her down the steps. As soon as they made contact, the electric sensation flowed between them and they let go.

"Ladies, I don't think there is any denying something special is happening. The rings. The book." Vivien looked meaningfully between Lorna and Heather. "Us."

Lorna shared a look with Heather as she handed Lorna's vodka and soda to her. Yes, she felt the connection. She looked at her ring as she held the cup. A bond was forming between them, as real as if someone had taken a sewing needle and stitched them together with invisible thread. "What does it mean? Why?"

"Julia said our pain joins us, and something about our heartaches calling to each other to be healed. We're meant to help each other. She disappeared and isn't saying more. Ghosts do that. Manifesting takes energy." Heather walked up the aisle as she continued to speak. "Every time we touch, I feel your pain. But more than that, I understand it. I feel the loss of your husband, Lorna, and the embarrassment it caused. You weren't allowed to grieve and can't take comfort in a lifetime of memories."

Heather ducked between the curtains leading toward the lobby. She automatically hooked the material over the holdback to keep the path open for the other two women.

"Viv, with you, I feel the emptiness left by Sam that you've never been able fill even though you try. You smile so brightly and laugh so loud to keep the world from seeing it. He was your great true love," Heather said. "And I don't have to say what you feel from me. I already know. I carry it every day. I think of him, my sweet Travis, whenever I see a playground, or hear the crack of a baseball bat, or breathe, or open my eyes. He's always there. I think the only way we're going to find out what all of this means is if we join hands and let whatever is happening, happen. I also think that once we do that there is no going back, so we better be ready to leap into the unknown."

"Oh, hey, you're all here."

Lorna turned at the sound of William's stunned voice. He came from the direction of the alley side door. When his eyes met hers, she saw his disbelief. He clearly hadn't been expecting to run into all three of them. She had to wonder why he was there, though. It was late and he had no reason to be in the theater.

Wait. He held a bottle of wine and flowers. Was he here for her?

"William, what are you doing here?" Heather asked.

"Did the two of you have a little..." Vivien took several steps toward William and gave a pointed look at what he carried. "William Warrick, did you bring Lorna sex wine?"

"What?" His eyes widened in surprise and he took a step back. He stared at Lorna. "No. Hold on a minute, no."

"William," Heather scolded. "What are you thinking? Lorna is a respectable woman."

"But—" He tried to protest.

"Seriously, William, respectable," Vivien insisted. "No chocolates? No strawberries and cream? Lorna is not some cheap booty call."

"Wait, no—" He looked helplessly at Lorna.

Lorna felt her cheeks heating slightly in embarrassment. It wouldn't have been so bad if she hadn't thought of William in the realm of a booty call on several late-night occasions. Even now, in his jeans and t-shirt, he looked terrific. Her heart did little flips in her stomach. He had clearly come to see her. That was the only reason he'd be here. She wondered if she should be worried or insulted by a man showing up late at night with wine and flowers. Was it presumptuous? Was that a standard dating ritual? She honestly didn't know. What she did know was that the flustered way he eyed her as the other two continued to tease him was endearing.

"Mom is going to be so disappointed in you, Will," Heather added. "You were raised better than this."

"Hey, now, just hold on," he argued. "This isn't that."

"So you don't like Lorna?" Vivien continued to torment the man. "That's kind of harsh. She said you asked her out on a date."

"I didn't say that," William countered. He made his way to Lorna and tried to hand her the wine and flowers. "It's not sex wine."

"So romantic," Vivien drawled before laughing.

"Okay, Viv, enough. Let's give him a break," Heather said, finally taking pity on her brother. "Lorna, we'll be upstairs if that's all right with you?"

"Yeah, sure, I'll be right there." Lorna slowly took the wine and flowers. The bouquet was an assorted mix of colors, the kind she'd find prearranged at a grocery store floral department.

William watched the others leave and didn't take his gaze from their direction until they heard foot-steps going up the stairs.

"Girls' night in," Lorna explained to break the awkward silence.

"What's with Heather's giant book?" He turned to look at her. "Little light reading?"

"Something like that. We found it in the theater," Lorna answered. "It looks like it belonged to your grandmother."

"Ah, I see." His gaze dipped to the floor. "Good ol' Grandma Julia."

She knew he didn't like talk of the supernatural and so decided not to press the topic. "What are you doing here?"

"I swear it isn't creepy. Looking at it now I was maybe misguided, but no creep intended. I saw your light on upstairs and thought I detected you moving around in your apartment when I glanced up from the street."

"We weren't upstairs. We were in the theater. If you saw someone, it wasn't me." Lorna might have left a light on by accident, but the fact he saw someone moving up there was disconcerting. Was Julia roaming her apartment?

"It was probably shadows from the headlights of a passing car," he dismissed, not even considering an otherworldly option. "I was going to sneak in and leave this for you to find in the morning. In my head it sounded sweet. Saying it out loud it sounds... yeah, a little creepy."

"We'll go with sweet," Lorna said, letting him off the hook. His sister and Vivien had picked on him enough.

"I appreciate that."

"I appreciate the gifts," Lorna said. "It was very *sweet* of you."

"When you say it like that the sweet sounds kind of girly." William gave a small laugh. "I don't think I'm winning any points tonight with this romantic gesture."

"I appreciate your very thought out, manly, dignified gift," Lorna amended. The fact that he admitted to his gesture being romantic sent a tiny wave of pleasure through her. It was always nice to be found attractive, especially by someone she liked.

"Thank you." William laughed harder as he ran his hand through his hair. "I mean, you're welcome. Wow, it's been a while since I've been tongue-tied around a beautiful woman. Any way I can get a second chance here? Maybe I can walk out and start this whole scene over?"

"You want me to call Viv and Heather back?" Lorna couldn't help teasing. William usually projected confidence and to see him like this was endearing.

"Oh, please no. Anyway, it looks like you all are in the middle of some womanly mischief. I won't keep you." William reached into his back pocket and pulled out a small card. He slipped it into her hand. Their fingers touched. His gaze dipped to her mouth for the briefest of seconds as if he thought about kissing her. She wished he would. With a small smile that reached his eyes, he backed away from her and said, "Just do me a favor. Give me a head start out the door before you let your friends read that and you all make fun of me."

"I'd never do that," Lorna said.

"I know." He turned to leave.

Lorna ran her finger under the small envelope's edge to open it. Pulling out the card, she read, *"Lorna, Just in case you decide not to show Thursday... Please reconsider, William."*

"I'll see you Thursday," Lorna called after him. He'd disappeared into the shadows leading toward the side door to the alley, so she wasn't sure if he'd heard her. She smiled toward the darkness as she leaned over to smell the flowers. They weren't fragrant, but that didn't matter. It had been a long time since anyone had given her flowers. Actually, the last time had been calla lilies from the funeral director.

The soft petals brushed her cheek and lips. She held them against her in an imaginary kiss as she continued to watch the shadows. Her tight self-control slipped a little. Knowing he liked her seemed to give her body permission to experience its attraction and she felt desire stirring within her.

William appeared outside, jogging across the street. She watched him through the front doors. When he made it to his truck, he glanced in the theater's direction and smiled. She wasn't sure if he saw her as she lifted her hand to give a small wave. He didn't return the gesture.

As he drove away, she curled her hand into a light fist. What was she doing? Nerves replaced the feelings of attraction. She'd come a long way in finding her independence but still didn't trust herself to be a good judge of character when it came to men.

Maybe she shouldn't go Thursday.

The flowers again brushed her cheek and she closed her eyes. The gesture seemed genuine and sweet. Not all men were Glenn. Surely her fake marriage had used up her ration of cosmic betrayal and she was owed something good, pure, *sweet*.

What were the odds she'd find two cheating jerks in the same lifetime?

Maybe she should go Thursday.

Maybe she shouldn't.

Should.

Shouldn't

Maybe she...

Crap. Perhaps she should just hide and never talk to any man ever again. That seemed to be the safest bet.

# CHAPTER SEVEN

"Pour me some more of that sex wine," Vivien said as she held her glass toward Lorna. She sat on a thick pillow on the floor across from where Heather and Lorna sat on the couch.

"Please stop calling it sex wine," Heather begged with a soft laugh. She'd refused to drink any of it, staying with her vodka.

"How are the hips, old lady?" Vivien asked. "Feeling better?"

Heather nodded. "Yeah, I'll be fine. I overdid it at a property renovation. I helped haul supplies up three stories and I'm feeling those five-gallon buckets of drywall plaster."

"That sounds awful. I'll stick to my treadmill," Vivien said.

"I'm more of a go-for-a-walk exerciser," Lorna admitted. "I never got into a gym routine."

Heather held the opened book on her lap. She'd been flipping through the pages. So far the front section had been a list of names, people who wanted to talk to dead loved ones and what they'd been willing to pay for the privilege. In the 1930s, the entries began to change. The requests became less about grieving parents and more about people trying to locate missing wills and trinkets. Since it was in the middle of the Great Depression, it was easy to understand that people had been desperate for money.

"William has good taste," Vivien said as Lorna poured more into the woman's stemless wine glass. "This bottle isn't the cheapest one in the store, that's for sure. He must really like you."

Lorna had not shown them the card. The other two had teased the man enough. When they asked, she just said he'd wanted to ask her out properly and left it at that.

Vivien stared into her glass. "I wonder what vodka chardonnay would taste like."

"And with that, you're now officially cut off," Heather decreed. To Lorna, she said, "When we were in high school—you know, drinking, um, *oh so legally* or whatnot—Viv decided to make beer floats. Cheap beer and vanilla ice cream."

"Ew." Lorna wrinkled her nose in disgust. "Dairy and beer don't sound like a good combination."

"Oh, it wasn't," Heather assured her, turning another page. "Not at all."

Vivien laughed, sliding off her pillow in her amusement. "I can't believe you all drank it. *Everyone* threw up that night. It was so gross." Her laughter died a little and she seemed lost in a memory as she whispered, "Man, I miss being young and stupid. Sam and I used to have the most fun."

"I miss being a mother," Heather said. "I miss being annoyed at four in the morning because someone had a nightmare."

"What about you, Lorna?" Vivien prompted. "What do you miss?"

"I miss..." Lorna rubbed the back of her neck. She never talked about this. No one had ever asked her to talk about it, at least not in a way that wasn't trolling for gossip. "I miss the idea of having someone to grow old with. I look in the mirror and see the age sneaking onto my face. I feel like all the wrinkles are in there just waiting to pop out. I don't feel ugly or old, just sad that I won't have someone with me who experienced what I looked like when I was twenty, or when I skinny-dipped in a lake, or when I was glowing and pregnant. I know it's silly, but I miss the possibility of that future. Even if I were to find someone again, *not* that I'm looking to remarry, I keep thinking that there is no way we'll have that seventieth anniversary together with the slide-show memories and all our grandkids and great-grandkids around us. No one else remembers Jennifer and Jacob teething at the same time, or Nicholas asking to give his brother a bath in the toilet. It makes me sad. I can tell the stories, but no one else will remember them with me."

"You never suspected him." Vivien's words were more of a statement than a question.

"Our marriage wasn't perfect. There were times when I thought about leaving Glenn, or hitting him with my car, or taking off on a separate vacation to get a break." Lorna felt tears welling in her eyes. She was so tired of crying about this. "I expected to grow old with my husband, rocking on the porch swing, talking about our legacy."

It was a simple dream, but one Lorna had carried in her heart. If she were honest with herself, she never took the time to consider if that was what she'd wanted out of life. Getting married, having children, and growing old was what the women in her family had always done. Her great-grandmother had been ninety-five when she died, and her grandmother eighty-seven. Her mother, still alive, was seventy-four. Judging by family history, she'd always expected to outlive her husband. Only, she hadn't expected to survive him so soon.

"Honestly, I would have said we had a good marriage before the end. It was only afterward that I discovered he had a second family," Lorna admitted.

"I'm so sorry," Heather said.

"I say we resurrect him and kick him in the balls," Vivien proposed. "You deserve an explanation and an apology."

For some reason, she found it easy to tell the story to Heather and Vivien. They didn't look at her in judgment. Their eyes didn't hold the accusation that she should have known. If anything, they appeared angry on her behalf.

"Actually, correction. We were the second family, not her," Lorna continued. "He married me second, which meant the first wife—the *true* wife, that's what Cheryl referred to herself as when we sat staring at each other across the conference table at the attorney's office—was his legal heir and had been entitled to everything."

"She came after your assets?" Vivien's brow furrowed.

Lorna nodded. "It was a mess. The police were called, but they determined quickly they couldn't do much since the polygamist was dead and there was no one to arrest. Then the probate court became involved. They wanted documents proving my belongings were mine. They dug through tax returns, and deeds, and... everything. The judge put little value in raising children when it came down to it. I wouldn't be surprised if it came out later that Cheryl bribed him. He seemed to think it was my fault I was the mistress whore with three..." Lorna choked back a tear. "Three illegitimate kids. That's what her lawyer called my babies."

"You weren't a mistress," Vivien stated firmly.

"You were married," Heather agreed. "You did nothing wrong. You entered into the union with the purest of intentions. Forget what the judge said, or that other woman and her asshole lawyer."

"What happened next?" Vivien prompted.

"It took time to untangle the web of lies. I couldn't afford the attorney it would take to try the case, and honestly, I didn't want more publicity. Cheryl didn't seem to mind it. She went on every newscast she could and painted herself as the victim, which made me one of the villains. She dragged her feet and made every step of the process excruciatingly long. I think she secretly wanted me to fight her in court. I even heard rumors she was shopping around for a book deal."

"You can bet none of us will be buying her crappy book," Vivien mumbled.

"When the dust settled, I found myself standing in the home that had been in my husband's name, with an eviction notice by the true wife." Lorna took a deep breath. "I had a yard sale, sold everything I could. Luckily, I had managed to pull money out of our joint accounts before Cheryl did her giant assets grab. After the eviction, I stayed with family, worked as a waitress, and saved up what I could with the knowledge that I wanted to leave Vermont and start my life over. Every friend and family member kept looking at me with such pity it was impossible to forget for even a moment what had happened. It's all anyone wanted to talk about."

"What about your children?" Heather lightly pushed a lock of Lorna's hair over her shoulder, careful not to make contact with her skin.

"They're angry. At first it was at me for not knowing. I think they felt too guilty about being angry at their father since he was dead, but it's getting better with time. They worry about me. The twins are in college. Jacob wanted to drop out and move back to help me. I wouldn't let him. Thankfully, the college funds were in their names and Cheryl couldn't touch them. Nicholas is living with a girlfriend."

"How did you come to pick this place?" Vivien reached for the bottle and poured more wine. The effects of liquor were beginning to show in her eyes but she held herself well.

"I was going through boxes looking for things I could sell and came across a picture of the beach that we'd taken on vacation. I remembered always wanting to come back to this town. The online job posting for a theater manager with room and board felt like a sign. I took all my cash, packed a couple of bags, hopped on a bus, and came here. Freewild Cove is my new start, my second chance at creating a life for myself."

"Freewild Cove and *William*," Vivien said with a small smile.

"He is pretty cute." Lorna wasn't sure what made her admit as much. She couldn't help but smile at the thought.

Heather turned back to the book on her lap and flipped through more pages. "Where were we?"

"Trying to decide if we hold hands or not," Vivien answered. "I still say yes. There's only one way to find out what happens and I want magic powers."

"And I still say we think before we leap," Heather said.

"Lorna?" Vivien asked.

"I'm still on the fence, wavering between scaredy-cat and what-the-hell-are-we-doing," Lorna admitted. "A week ago I wouldn't have thought psychic finding abilities were a real thing, and now..."

She gestured at the book. How could she deny something supernatural was happening here? There was no other explanation for how she could have known to reach between two curtains, to a hidden lever that opened up the floor, to discover a lost altar and mysterious séance book that had been hidden away for over half a century.

Heather set the open book on the oval coffee table.

Lorna leaned forward to study it. She turned through several of the pages. Were all of these names real ghosts that Julia had contacted? Was it genuine, or a spiritualist scam? She'd seen scary movies with fake mediums in them before. She wanted to believe there was more out there. She wanted to believe her new friends weren't certifiable. Most of all, she wanted to trust what she was feeling.

She ran her index finger along the edge of the pages and imagined she felt the hum of power inside the words. She flipped it open to one of the back pages. A drawing of a plant illustrated a page on how to make a smudging stick with sage and lavender. "It's not all séances." Lorna turned to the next page to find candle making directions. "There's craft instructions in here too."

"What are we meant to do with this?" Vivien asked.

"Sell homemade candles?" Lorna suggested, not really serious.

Vivien didn't laugh. "I meant with the séances. Do you think we need to write who we want to contact down in the ledger and then they appear?" She reached for the wine bottle for another refill. "I wish we could find an instruction manual."

"I'll see what I can do." Lorna closed the book and moved her finger an inch down the width of the book and then reopened it by turning several pages at once. Vivien pushed upon her knees to get a better look at the page Lorna had chosen. Heather leaned forward. On the page was an illustration of the book cover with three hands resting flat on top, touching to form a triangle over the symbols. Each hand had a ring that matched theirs. Images of lit candles were drawn in the corners of the page.

"Do you feel that?" Vivien whispered. "The temperature just dropped."

The curtains fluttered, and they all gasped, turning toward the noise. The window wasn't open and yet the material blew into the room like it was.

"Grandma?" Heather asked. "Is that you?"

They waited, listening and watching. The curtains settled. The apartment lights flickered before going out.

"Is it Julia?" Vivien asked.

"I don't hear her," Heather said. "Maybe the air conditioner kicked on and blew a fuse."

"I don't like this," Lorna whispered into the darkness. Streetlights from outside should have made it easier to see but it felt like something blocked the light from entering the apartment. She gave a nervous laugh. "I think I'm starting to freak myself out."

Lorna reached to the side table and fumbled for a candle lighter. Finding it, she pulled the trigger and lit the flame, instantly bringing it to a candlewick.

"Do you have a flash—" Heather began, only to be cut off when the candle flame ignited.

As the fire burst over the wick, every candle in the apartment lit itself to cast the room in a soft glow.

"—light," Heather finished weakly.

Lorna peered at the candles and had the distinct feeling they were no longer alone. The air had a heaviness to it, pressing down on them.

"Flashlight?" Heather repeated.

"Apothecary cabinet," Lorna answered, not getting up to retrieve her emergency flashlight. Her heart beat fast and she wasn't sure she could move from the couch. The trembling in her limbs made it impossible to stand. "Bottom left corner drawer."

"I'll get it." Vivien hurried across the room.

Lorna moved the candle she'd lit next to the book. She slowly turned the page and found paragraphs of handwritten text unlike the séance lists that came before. She silently read, "*Spirits tethered to this plane we humbly seek your guidance. Spirits search amongst your numbers for a lost child, we call forth...*" A blank space was left between the words. "*...from the great beyond.*"

Vivien had asked for instructions and it looked like Lorna had found them. Her eyes moved to the next section.

"*Spirits tethered to this plane we command you to join us...*"

And to the next section.

*"We open the door between two worlds to call forth the spirit of..."* Another blank spot. *"Come back from the grave so that we may hear. Come back from the grave and show yourself to us so that all may see. Come back from the grave and answer for what you have done so that you may be judged."*

And still the next.

*"Beings tethered to this plane, full of rage and filled with pain. We call you to come near. We call you to face what you fear. We call you to your eternal hell. Pay the price with this final knell."*

"What do you both make of this?" Heather asked.

Lorna rubbed her arms and reached for her drink. "It's pretty heavy stuff."

"Let me see." Vivien produced a pair of reading glasses from her purse on the floor. She sat next to Lorna on the couch, forcing her to slide over to make room, and then shone the flashlight at the coffee table to make it easier to see.

The next entry on the page read, *"Spirit you have been found pure. We release you into the light. Go in peace and love."*

Vivien placed her hand on the page, blocking

Lorna from reading more. "We can use these to call spirits. We should hold a séance."

"And talk to who?" Heather asked.

"Julia? We know she's here," Vivien suggested. "She could tell us why she gave us the rings and how all of this works."

"I don't see her around," Heather said. "I'm starting to get the impression that she's avoiding me."

"All the more reason to call her up on the psychic telephone," Vivien said.

"I don't know if we should until we know what we're doing. There has to be a price that comes from meddling." Heather brushed Vivien's hand aside, only making brief contact. She turned the page as if to continue reading. "Some things are better left alone."

"Heather, don't you see what this means? This proves we were right. There is magic in the world. I can talk to Sam," Vivien said, her voice a little breathless. "I would give anything to see him again, to hear him. Julia said we were brought together to heal each other's pain. Maybe this is how we do that."

Lorna always wanted to ask Glenn why he'd done it. Now she could. All she had to do was believe in the signs she'd been experiencing since Vivien had first introduced herself.

"Heather? Don't you want to see Travis?" Vivien persisted. "You said that he never came to you after his... after."

Heather looked as if someone had just tried to hit her with a car. She covered her mouth with her hand. Moisture gathered in her eyes.

The wind kicked up again, blowing from the closed window. The candles flickered. A gust hit all three of them, swirling around the apartment to come from multiple directions. Hair whipped around Lorna's head, lashing her face and stinging her with each tiny pelt. It blocked her eyes so she couldn't see. Next to her she felt Vivien and Heather struggling against the unseen force. Heather's elbow bumped Lorna's cheek.

"What the hell," Vivien swore.

The wind stopped. Lorna managed to push the hair out of her face. All the candles were out. Vivien shone the flashlight around the room to look for clues.

"The book!" Heather snatched the book from the table and began shaking it. Red droplets rained from within.

Vivien's wine glass had tipped over onto the pages and spilled across the coffee table to drip on the rug. Lorna hurried to the kitchen and grabbed a dry towel. Vivien shone the light after her to help.

"Here." Lorna held the towel and blotted at the book before attending to her rug and coffee table.

"How is it?" Vivien picked up her reading glasses from the floor where they must have fallen.

"Some of the ink is smeared," Heather answered.

"Leave it open and set it on the counter to dry," Vivien said. "We might be able to save the pages."

"What was that?" Lorna asked. "Where did that wind come from?"

"Maybe the three of us were sitting too close," Vivien suggested, though her tone lacked conviction. "It's like when we touch. Maybe we bumped each other or something."

"Maybe." Heather also sounded doubtful as she placed the book on the kitchen counter. "I'm going to check the fuse box."

Lorna dropped the wet towel in the kitchen sink before nervously moving over to the window. Her hand trembled as she touched the curtains that had been blowing. They were much cooler than the rest of the room. Pushing them aside, she looked to the street below.

William's truck was back, parked across the street,

but she couldn't see him inside the cab. She glanced down the sidewalk. A couple came out of the Chinese restaurant and walked in the opposite direction.

"Do you see anything?" Vivien asked.

"William's truck is back," Lorna answered, "but I don't see him."

The lights came on. Heather closed the fuse box on the wall with a decisive metal clang. Vivien turned off the flashlight but didn't set it down.

"That was weird." Heather crossed the room toward them. "I think maybe I've had too much to drink. I usually don't spook this easily."

"You wouldn't be the only one." Lorna again peered down at the street. What was William doing back?

Shadows and darkness had a way of inspiring dread. The apartment didn't feel as scary with the lights on.

"We need food to soak up the alcohol," Vivien decided.

"Can we raid your fridge?" Heather asked.

"Yeah, but if you find food, I really will believe in magic. I haven't been to the grocery store," Lorna answered. "Shopping day is tomorrow or today? What time is it anyway?"

Heather peered inside, only to announce, "We have coffee creamer and green pepper jelly."

"Oh, I got an idea." Vivien grabbed her phone and dialed. It wasn't long before she received an answer. "Hey, William, I have a very important favor to ask." She paused, but Lorna couldn't hear what he was saying on the other end. "No. I don't need bail money again but thanks for reminding me of that. I need you to stop pining all lovesick outside of Lorna's apartment like a stalker, and run down the street to pick us up some sesame chicken, and—" She directed a childish expression at the phone. "Oh, good, see, you're already there. Perfect. And yes, we may be a little drunk. Thanks for the sex wine, by the way. Now listen. This is important. Sesame chicken, broccoli and beef, sweet and sour shrimp, ginger chicken, um…"

When Vivien glanced at her, Lorna said, "Crab Rangoon?"

"Crab Rangoon." Vivien glanced at Heather.

"Pork dumplings," Heather added. "Chitterlings."

"Pork dumplings," Vivien repeated, "and… what is a chitterling?" William must have answered because Vivien scrunched up her face and shook her head. "Oh, hell, no. Just add a bunch of fried rice and fortune cookies and whatever else looks good. We are starving. Thanks, Will, you're a lifesaver, use your key to get in and bring it up."

Vivien quickly ended the call without giving William enough time to refuse.

"Chitterling? Seriously?" Vivien shook her head at Heather. "What is wrong with you?"

"Don't knock it until you try it," Heather quipped.

"Oh, I'm knocking, and I'm definitely not trying." Vivien gave a light shiver to prove her disgust.

"We don't have to make him bring us all of that. I can run across and grab our order," Lorna offered.

"He'll be fine. Trust me. This will be the most excitement he's had in a month," Vivien dismissed. "Plus, I think he's happy for an excuse to come over." She winked at Lorna.

"What about...?" Heather began.

They all turned in unison to the book.

"I think we should try it." Vivien took a roll of paper towels from the counter. She tore off a square and placed it on the damp page before closing the book. Then going to Lorna's kitchen table, she pushed aside a decorative bowl with balls of twine to set the book down. She rested her hand on the cover. "Before William gets here. That way, we'll have help on the way if anything weird happens. And if nothing happens, we'll all have a good laugh about it."

"I don't think this is a good idea," Heather said. "We should put it back where we found it and forget we ever saw it."

"Heather, please," Vivien pleaded. "I miss Sam so much. If there is a chance that I can see him again, I have to try."

Without removing her hand from the book, Vivien took a seat. Her ring laid close to the matching symbol on the cover.

Lorna couldn't explain why, but she found herself sitting down and reaching for the book. She placed her hand next to Vivien's, forming one point of the triangle. Energy pulsed through her causing excitement and fear.

"I want to hear what Glenn has to say for himself," Lorna said. "I want to know if I was a blind fool before I try dating again. I don't know if I can trust myself. We can remove our hands and end it at any time."

Heather took a seat. She stared at the book, not touching it.

Lorna felt Vivien's longing for her lost love. The ache came in through her fingers on the book and trailed up her arm, as profound as any emotion she'd ever felt.

That wasn't all. The book amplified her longing for answers. She stopped worrying about what might happen and became focused on what she wanted, which was for Glenn to answer for what he did to her and their children.

Heather hovered her hand over the book. "I don't want to contact my son. Not right now. Not after I've been drinking. I'm not ready." Tears entered her eyes and she took several deep breaths. "I don't think I can..."

"Okay, we won't," Vivien assured her. "We would never force that on you."

Heather nodded and lowered her hand.

The instant Heather made contact, Lorna stiffened, her elbow locking into place. The energy became almost painful as it shot up her arm. She felt the hair lifting from her shoulders. Her palm began to burn.

"Someone say something," Vivien said. "What did the book say?"

"Ah...?" Heather shook her head, trying to remember.

Candles lit by themselves, flaming high before settling.

"That was cool," Vivien whispered.

"We should have written down what we needed to say," Lorna said. "Is it too late to start over?"

"The ink is smeared," Vivien said. "We have the basic idea. Let's wing it. Worst case scenario it doesn't work."

"Worst case scenario we open a portal to hell and call out a demon or something," Lorna disagreed.

"Don't think like that," Heather scolded. "Focus on what you want."

"Okay, I think it went something like, we open the door between two worlds?" Lorna knew this was maybe not the smartest plan, yet somehow the words eased any lingering fear. The nearness of the others gave her strength. She felt the power running through her, dulling her senses, whispering that it was going to be all right. She felt her new friends with her and didn't want to stop.

Heather nodded. "Yes, that's it. We open the door between two worlds and call forth the tethered spirits of Sam and Glenn. Come back to us from the grave so that we may hear you speak."

The book began to shake. A tapping noise sounded as if coming from far away.

"Come back from the grave so that all may see." Lorna felt her arm being lifted as the book levitated from the table. Her eyes met Heather and Vivien's. "Come back from the grave and tell me why…"

Lorna couldn't remember the rest. One of the incantations had said something about facing judgment. Another tried to give peace.

"I want answers, Glenn," Lorna blurted. "Give me answers."

"Sam?" Vivien called. "Are you with us? Can you hear me?"

"You must be drunk."

At the sound of the male voice Lorna gasped in fright and jerked her hand away. She hadn't meant to, but it was too late to take back. The book slammed down on the table. She jumped again at the heavy thud. Her heart beat fast and she shared a wide-eyed look with Heather and Vivien. No one spoke.

"You called me. I'm William, not Sam." William appeared at the top of the stairs. "I knocked but no one answered so I hope it's all right that I just walked in. I take it you still want this food?"

Heather gave a small laugh of surprise to see it was her brother. Lorna's heart was still pounding and she barely managed a half smile.

William came toward the kitchen counter carrying two large bags of food. "Someone owes me fifty dollars plus a tip for the delivery."

"Oh, ah..." Lorna glanced at the bags and then around the apartment for her purse.

Vivien touched her arm to stop her. A tiny electrical snap jolted them at the contact and Vivien instantly let go. "He's joking."

Lorna rubbed her arm.

"She's right. I'm teasing." William set down the bags and then looked at the book on the table. He started to move toward it. "How's book club?"

"Enlightening," Vivien answered, taking the book and moving it across the studio apartment to set it on Lorna's bed where he couldn't see it as well.

Lorna glanced around the apartment for signs of ghosts. There were none.

"I'll get plates." Heather went to the kitchen.

William pulled water bottles out of the food bags and set them on the counter where they could see them. "Make sure you ladies hydrate. That's half the battle when it comes to hangovers."

He turned to leave.

Lorna still felt strange. Being alone with Heather and Vivien had given her a sense of euphoria and caused her to act recklessly. Somehow William walking in had brought sanity back into the room. How else could she explain saying yes to summoning her dead husband while drunk? Heather had been right. They had no clue what they were messing with.

"Have you eaten? Do you want to join us?" Lorna pushed up from the table, not wanting William to leave. If he went, they surely pick up where they left off and she wasn't certain she was ready for that. If Vivien begged them to summon Sam, how could Lorna say no? She knew how much pain the other woman was in.

"Yes, stay," Heather insisted.

"We interrupted your dinner," Vivien added.

Or maybe none of them were ready to try again.

"I don't want to intrude upon girls' night." William hesitated. "I can go—"

"No," Heather and Vivien shot in unison, cutting him off.

"Please, stay," Lorna added.

He took several steps back toward them and stopped. "Are you ladies all right? You seem..."

"Drunk?" Vivien offered. "Yep. We are."

"I was going to say worried," William corrected.

"Worried that... the food is going to get cold," Vivien ineloquently said as she pointed at the bags. "Bring those bad boys over here."

William sighed and shook his head slightly as he did as Vivien commanded. "Keep ordering me around like this, Viv, and I won't come to your rescue next time."

"Sure you will," Vivien answered, moving around the table to take a seat near the windows. "You always say that and then you always do. You have to love me. I'm practically like a sister to you."

"I begged my mom not to adopt you," he mumbled loud enough for her to hear.

"I begged my mom for a puppy named Will," Vivien retorted.

"Stop it, both of you." Heather interrupted their playful argument. "Lorna's going to think you're serious."

Lorna didn't say anything as they bantered. They had known each other for a long time and it showed. That history was embedded in every movement, every teasing word. They didn't mean to isolate her with their playfulness, but they did. She had to wonder why Vivien and William weren't together. They had a natural rhythm between them. Most relationships were built on friendship.

William sat down next to Lorna at the table. He leaned into her and whispered, "Are you sure this is all right? I don't want to intrude."

Lorna nodded. "Yes. The more the merrier. We invited you, how's that intruding?"

Her eyes drifted behind him, once again searching for signs of the supernatural. So much for being a brave, independent woman. Levitating books and self-lighting candles might be super cool in theory but seeing it firsthand was also terrifying. There was no way she wanted to be left alone in the apartment. She'd take all the company she could get.

CHAPTER EIGHT

Soft, unfamiliar sounds and bright sunlight welcomed Lorna to a new day. She lay on her couch barely able to focus on the edge of her coffee table. Her eyes were dry and she realized she'd slept in her contacts. She blinked several times for moisture. It didn't take long for the evening's events to come rushing back. Heather and Vivien had slept in the bed, which left her the couch. The stiff back was worth not spending the night alone in her apartment.

She reached for the coffee table and touched the surface. Her fingers adhered to the sticky wine residue. The sluggish ache in her body and dullness in her head were to be expected from a hangover, only the amount she'd drank couldn't account for what she felt.

When the magic—because what else could she call what had happened but magical—coursed through her, she'd felt powerful, exhilarated. It took her mind to a place where logic didn't matter as much as feelings. Since the moment she'd put on the ring, it had been building inside her.

Heather's pain from the loss of her son. Vivien's loneliness from missing her dead husband. And Lorna's shame that needed answers. They were all three of them stuck in the past, and their individual losses controlled them.

Pain had brought them together. Julia Warrick had told Heather as much. Lorna knew it to be true. This new friendship could be the key to unlocking the door that kept them trapped in their saddest moments.

They could say, *"Goodbye."*

They could say, *"I love you."*

They could say, *"Damn you, Glenn, for your betrayal."*

A sound in the kitchen caused her to shift her hazy focus. She saw the door to her side-by-side fridge hanging open, only to close slowly.

Lorna pushed up from the couch to see past the island. William held a rag and swiped it along the surface of the countertop. His eyes met hers and he smiled.

"I cleaned up and put the leftovers in the fridge," he said, his voice soft as he glanced toward her bedroom as if not to wake the others. He turned his back for a moment, and she ran her fingers quickly through her hair to straighten the locks before he again faced her with a lidded coffee cup from the shop down the block. He walked it toward her. "I thought you might need this."

"You came all the way back here to bring us coffees?" Lorna asked in surprise as she took it. "Are you trying for sainthood?"

"It wasn't too far. I walked down the street this morning when they opened. I slept downstairs last night. There's a cot in the back storage that the old projectionist used to nap on during his shifts," William said. "It was late and I didn't feel like driving home. Ace kept me company. He slept on my chest."

Lorna sipped the latte and made a sound of appreciation. "Mm, well I for one am grateful you didn't leave."

He again glanced toward the bed and gestured to the stairs. Lorna slipped the blankets off her lap so she could follow him. She drew her hand along the wall to steady herself. The faintest trace of his cologne drifted behind him. She wore fluffy pink socks from the night before and had to tread carefully to keep from slipping on the wooden stairs. When they made it down, she shut the door behind her.

"I'll be right back." Lorna moved past him to go to the restroom, pausing only long enough to set her coffee on the concession counter.

She soon found herself staring into the mirror as she washed her hands. Ten years ago she would have made an excuse to run to the bathroom to put on makeup and make herself presentable. There was still that part of her that didn't want this to be the image she showed William. She splashed cold water on her face and rubbed at her dry eyes with moist fingers to force the contacts to move. Then she pinched her cheeks in some arcane effort to look less sleep deprived. It didn't work.

Lorna sighed. Then again, who cared?

Lorna gave a small laugh and stopped what she was doing. She was an adult and this is what a forty-four-year-old woman looked like in the early morning.

What was it the internet people always joked? *I'm middle-aged and I have no more fucks to give.*

That was probably one of the aptest sayings she'd

ever heard.

Lorna left the restroom expecting to see William waiting for her. He wasn't there. She heard a noise near the office and went to see where he'd gone.

"William?"

The office lights weren't on. She paused to look inside the dark room. The temperature felt lower like it had before when Julia had been in the room. The shadows appeared to shift, and she instantly went to flip the light switch. Lorna looked at the corner. Nothing was there. The creepy feeling from the night before resurfaced.

"Grandma Julia?" Lorna asked the empty office. "If that's you can you give me a sign? Can you show yourself?"

Lorna wasn't sure if it was relief or disappointment that filled her when a spirit didn't materialize. She turned off the lights and slowly backed away from the door.

Hearing a noise coming from the storage area, she changed routes to check for William. It sounded like someone slid boxes along the floor.

She opened the door. "Can I help you find something? I rearranged all the—"

The noises stopped. The storage room was dark.

"Hello?" She called. "Is someone in here?"

No answer.

"Ace?" she whispered, hoping it was as simple as that. "Kitty are you hiding in here?"

"Lorna? Who are you talking to?" William asked behind her.

Lorna gave a small jolt of surprise and spun around to face him. She let go of the door, allowing its weight to pull it shut. "Where were you?"

"Sitting in the theater drinking my coffee," he answered. "Can I help you get something out of storage?"

He pushed open the door and turned on the light to investigate who she'd been talking to. Lorna glanced around. There was no one. However, a box sat in the middle of the room where it didn't belong.

Not wanting to admit she'd been scaring herself after a night of ghost talk, she asked, "Did you see the stage floor? I don't know how we're going to fix that hole."

"I didn't notice a hole. What happened? Did the floor crack? This building is old, but the stage has always appeared solid."

"You didn't see it? It's a giant hole in the middle of the stage. You can't miss it," she answered.

William gave her a quizzical look before he made his way toward the theater. "Does my sister have help coming to fix it? She mentioned you all were fully booked for the next few months. I have to put together some paperwork today for the bank, but I can come back later with my tools."

"We have some indie film screening set up for the first of the week," Lorna said. "But after that, yeah, people will need to get on there. A director has us booked for auditions. He's shooting a movie not far from here in a few months."

"Are you going to audition? Become a movie star?" William went to look at the stage.

Lorna followed him as he outpaced her, studying him as he walked up the stairs ahead of her. "I think my days starring in a string bikini on the beach are past me."

"I don't know." He gave a quick smile. "I'd watch that."

Lorna nearly choked on a laugh at the flirtation. She had set him up for it without thinking. It only proved how out of practice she was when it came to dating.

"I don't see anything," he said.

"How can you miss it?" Lorna frowned. Even as she asked the question, she noticed the floor looked flat from where she stood. She joined him on the stage. The hole had been repaired. The night before the mechanism had been broken, and the altar had rolled over the section of lowered floorboards. It would've taken some effort to get the floor out from underneath it. "I don't understand. Did you...?"

"I didn't do anything." William walked along the stage, looking down as if he'd find what she was talking about.

Lorna stood on the edge of where the giant hole had been and touched the floor with her toe. She put her weight slowly forward to see if it would move. It felt firm as if nothing had happened. Frowning, she went to the curtains where the levers had been. They were still there.

"Don't move," she instructed so he wouldn't fall through. She flipped the lever, but nothing happened.

"Am I waiting for something?" He gave a small laugh.

"I don't..." Lorna reached to try the two remaining levers, flipping them up and down multiple times. She listened for the sound of vibrations to come up through the stage. She dropped her hand to her side and frowned. "My mistake. Heather must have already taken care of it."

Only, Heather had been with her the entire night.

She rubbed her eyes. It had been real. It happened.

Lorna had seen the broken pullies and old cogs beneath the stage. She'd felt the dirty floor against her hands and knees as she crawled to retrieve the book. Whatever had been in place to retract the altar had long ago deteriorated and stopped working. There was no reason why the stage should be fixed.

William strode toward her. Lorna cringed as he stepped over the hole's location, but he made it across without the floor buckling beneath him. He stopped about a foot away from where she stood next to the curtain.

"You seem..." He hesitated as he studied her. "Did my sister and Vivien tell you the family ghost stories last night? Is that what they were doing with that old book? I can't help but notice you seem jumpy this morning, and I'm hoping it has nothing to do with me showing up with coffee."

"It's not you," Lorna assured him. He'd made it clear how he felt about his family's history with spirits, and she didn't feel comfortable answering the rest of his questions. Also, she couldn't help but wonder how many of those spirits were watching them right now.

She glanced out over the empty seats. What if all

of them were filled with ghosts watching them—the living—like a play? Most of the seats had springs that retracted them back to make room for walking, but a few were broken. Those few were on her to-do list to fix and didn't stay up no matter how many times she tightened and replaced the bolts. What if that was where Julia Warrick and her spirit friends sat?

"You'd tell me if I was making you uncomfortable or coming on too strong, right?" William's voice disrupted her thoughts, drawing her gaze back to his. "Because, despite what my sister's troublemaker of a friend may have told you about me, I'm not some smooth player with a different date every night."

"She said you were a nice guy," Lorna answered. Well, the word Vivien had repeatedly used was *hot*. Yes, William was hot and sexy and had the kind of eyes that drew her attention. She wasn't sure how to say such a thing, or even if she should. "And something about you being a fan of pleather couches, the ones that have cup holders in the arms."

"Hey, now, don't make fun of my couch," William defended. "It's comfortable and keeps me from spilling my drinks. Plus it reclines."

Lorna lifted her hands between them as if to keep him back. "I wouldn't dare come between a man and his couch."

That sounded a tad dirtier than she'd intended. She pretended not to notice.

"Is there something between you and Vivien?" Lorna needed to know. "Or was there? The two of you put off a vibe."

"No, and never. We've all been friends for a long time and have been through life's trials together, but there was never anything remotely romantic going on." William's lips curled up at the side in a sheepish smile. His hand rested on her upper arm, forcing her mind to focus on his touch. She dropped her arms at the contact. "In case it isn't completely obvious, Lorna Addams, I like *you* in a romantic way. I want to get to know you better."

Lorna's heart quickened by small degrees. She wasn't some schoolgirl with a crush. Butterflies didn't generally flutter around in her stomach at the thought of being next to a man. She knew what sexual attraction was. Most of the time it was that annoying ache that argued with all the logical thoughts in her head. She looked at his light grip on her arm. He had the rough fingers of a man who worked with his hands. There was a fantasy somewhere in that fact alone.

Silence filled the theater like the captured breath of an audience waiting for the climactic final act. She felt as if they were watched, rapt eyes looking at every detail of what they did. A shiver worked its way over her, covering her skin with goosebumps. She was an actress who didn't know her lines, didn't know how to push this story thread forward.

Thoughts raced through her mind, crowding the single moment. It had been a long time since she'd kissed someone who wasn't Glenn. They'd been together most of her adult life. Those moments were part of her, sprinkled throughout her existence in impressions and memories. That knowledge kept her frozen in place and unable to act on her impulses with William.

For years, she'd told herself that what she wanted didn't matter. She was a mother. She was a wife. She was the glue that kept the family together, the oil that kept it running smoothly, the tonic that kept them healthy and safe. She was what everyone else needed her to be. She was endless dinners and rides to school. She absorbed their pains, healed their wounds, loved them unconditionally. She took very little for herself. It had never been her intention to sound like a martyr. It all happened so slowly, piece by piece until she forgot who she was without them.

But her children were grown, and her husband was dead. She no longer needed to be all those things. She could shed that skin and become some-thing new, *someone* new.

New.

The future had no road map. There was no porch swing for reminiscing. The home she'd raised her children in no longer belonged to her.

New.

Terrifying.

Exciting.

The next chapter.

Her second chance to live a new life.

New Lorna could kiss William, or in the very least allow him to kiss her.

William apparently had no such inner struggle. When her eyes moved up to meet his, he leaned forward. His intent was clear, and he gave her plenty of time to react and pull away. His hand moved from her arm to cup her cheek, quietly asking permission.

Lorna's heartbeat quickened. His gentle kiss barely had time to settle before a slow clap sounded from the invisible audience. She gasped in surprise and pulled away. Her eyes went to the seats, not seeing anyone.

"Did you hear that?" she asked.

William grumbled and turned to the chairs.

Loudly, he stated, "Vivien, I know that's you. Stop acting like a teenager."

Lorna briefly touched her lips. They tingled and she wanted him to continue.

"I'm sorry, where were we?" He cupped her cheek and moved to resume his kiss. This time he deepened the pressure, parting his lips so that his tongue could slip along the seam of her mouth. A light moan left her.

"William? Are you in here?" Heather yelled from the back.

Lorna pulled away first at the sound.

William closed his eyes and frowned. "Yes, sis?"

Heather appeared slowly from between the curtains searching for them. "Oh, there you are. We were thinking of going to get breakfast. Is Lorna with you?"

"You're leaving?" Lorna came from behind William.

"Vivien wants pancakes and I need to pick up some tools to fix the stage." Heather slowly walked down the aisle toward them. "I'll be back in an hour... unless you need me to stay away longer?"

"I don't see anything wrong with the stage," William stated. Whatever the moment had been between them had gone with Heather's interruption. Lorna wished they could get it back.

"Yeah, if you don't mind ballerinas dancing their way into a crater." Heather chuckled, coming closer. "I'm pretty sure my insurance will frown about that."

He looked down at the floor and tapped at the boards with the heel of his boot. "What am I missing?"

"Seriously?" Heather came closer. Her eyes went to the stage, and she frowned. She looked up in question.

Lorna shrugged from behind William and mouthed, "I don't know."

Heather hurried up the stairs and began the same process Lorna had gone through, pressing around the place the hole had been with her foot.

"Are you sure you weren't doing anything more than drinking last night?" William teased. "Maybe grandma left a little wacky tobaccy with her book?"

"You're hilarious," Heather muttered.

"I'm not the one seeing holes where there are none," William said.

"I saw it too," Lorna put forth. "There's a lever that opened up to a secret area underneath the floor with a..."

He gave her a bemused look.

"It happened," Lorna insisted. "There are a series of pullies and tracks under the stage."

"What all did my sister tell you about Grandma Julia?" William asked Lorna.

Heather waved at him in dismissal, indicating she wasn't paying attention to him as she went to where Lorna had discovered the levers.

"Not only did Julia charge for séances," William continued, "she bootlegged moonshine and grew marijuana during Prohibition. That's how she made enough money to build this theater and several of the other Warrick properties in town. Our Julia was quite the outlaw."

Heather slapped her hand against the post with the levers.

"I think she sounds like an amazing, strong, intelligent, fascinating woman," Lorna answered. She liked William, and there was no denying her attraction to him, but his pigheadedness on the topic of all things Julia-related bordered on annoying.

"She was all those things," Heather agreed.

"I wish I could have known her," Lorna added, wondering if Julia's spirit could hear them talking. "I can't imagine what it must have been like to be a woman in the 1920s, forging her own way in not only a man's world but during the Great Depression, and commissioning buildings, and running a theater."

"She ran a hotel too," Heather added, "but it burned down in the fifties."

"Foul play?" Lorna asked.

Heather shrugged.

"I think you misunderstand the point I was trying to make," William said. "All pot-smoking jokes aside, bootleggers were known to have hidden stashes, secret compartments, heck, even secret tunnels and rooms. So, if you're telling me that Julia rigged some kind of hidden contraption that made the bottom of the stage open up, I'm inclined to believe you. What was down there?"

Lorna shared a look with Heather.

"A ledger of her séances, people she contacted, what she charged, stuff like that," Heather said.

"The book you were reading last night," William concluded.

"It was with that old altar from those photographs that Dad had of her," Heather said. "The altar is still down there."

"That's why you looked spooked." William gave a long sigh and ran his fingers through his hair. "You weren't just reading that old ledger, were you?" His gaze went to where Heather touched her ring and then to Lorna's hand. "Those belonged to Julia, didn't they? Vivien had a ring too. I thought they looked familiar. Julia had a whole box of those when we were little. You're meddling with that stuff."

"What do you care?" Heather asked. "You don't believe it's real. Isn't that what you're always telling people? By your logic, if it's not real, then there is no harm in what we're doing."

"Heather..." William looked like he wanted to plead with her but stopped himself. "I have to get some papers together for work. I'll see you later. Let me know if you need help figuring out the floor." To Lorna, he added, "I hope to see you Thursday, if not before."

Lorna nodded. "I'll be there."

"Good." His smile was well-meaning, but it didn't reach his eyes as he turned away to hop off the stage and make his way up the aisle. He didn't look back as he left.

"He used to see them," Heather said softly as she came to stand by Lorna. "When he was little, he saw ghosts, but he grew out of it. My mother tried to convince him it was imaginary friends, but I think he knows the truth deep down, even if he can no longer see them for himself. I also think it scares him."

"Is Julia here?" Lorna asked, looking around at the chairs.

"I don't see her," Heather answered. She motioned for Lorna to follow her as she stepped down from the stage.

"Last night, do you think we...?"

Heather gave a short laugh. "I think we drank too much. I think we took a little too many creative liberties with holding a séance. And I think the only thing we summoned was a hangover and the heebie-jeebies, which can both be cured with coffee and carbs."

"So, no one else is here?"

"Not that I see," Heather said. She led the way from the stage, moving up the aisle.

Lorna glanced to where she'd seen Heather say hello to her grandmother. "Were they here when you walked in?"

"Not that I saw."

"Are you sure?" She'd felt like people were watching her when she was with William on the stage.

"I didn't see any."

Lorna opened her mouth to ask more, but Heather stopped walking, turned around, and lifted her hand.

"It's not a parlor trick or party game," Heather stated. She took a deep breath as if policing her tone. "I know what you and Vivien want from me, and I'm sorry, I can't force it to happen for you. I couldn't make it happen for *me*. I looked everywhere for my son until it ended the tiny shreds of my marriage that had survived his death. I don't tell people what I can do because I don't want to spend the rest of my life answering whether or not I see spirits."

What a horrible side effect of such a skill, to be reminded constantly of death—especially after the death of a child. That's not something Lorna had considered when faced with the idea of séances and ghosts. She'd thought of her own selfish need to confront the past. They'd been rash and foolish the night before, playing around with things they didn't understand. Why hadn't that fear been there while they were doing it? It's almost like a spell had been cast over them, forcing them to throw caution to the wind.

"I won't ask again," Lorna said. "You're right, and I'm sorry. Vivien and I should not have pushed last night. I don't think of you like some grinder monkey ready to perform tricks on command. If that's what it felt like, I apologize. The two of you are the only friends I have here. Actually, the only friends I have anywhere. You don't treat me like a novelty, or a dumbass. I value that and don't want to lose it. All I know about ghosts comes from the horror movies my kids used to watch with their friends and from decorating for Halloween. I don't know how any of this works in real life. What we did, or tried to do, has left me on shaky ground."

"Thank you for understanding." Heather reached for the curtain in the doorway before turning to see what she was doing. Her hand bumped the wall and she yelped in surprise. She jerked her hand back.

"Are you all right? What happened?" Lorna asked as Heather cradled her hand.

"I cut myself on something." Heather clenched her fist.

Lorna went to check and found that the curtain holdback had broken off the wall. It left behind a sharp protrusion of plastic.

"When did that happen? It wasn't like that during the recital." Lorna frowned.

"I'm glad I found it and not one of the customers." Heather opened her hand to examine the cut. It had sliced her palm. "I don't think it's too deep."

"Let me get you something for the bleeding."

Lorna ran ahead of her to the napkin dispensers. They were the closest option. "Here, let me see it. You might need stitches."

"It'll be fine. Working on job sites, I keep my tetanus shot up to date. If it's bad, I'll just superglue it together and save the six-hundred-dollar emergency room fee."

Lorna pressed napkins into Heather's palm, dabbing at the cut. "At least let me clean it for you."

With two boys and a girl who could outplay her brothers, Lorna was a pro at doctoring cuts and bruises. She placed the bloody napkins on the glass case and grabbed clean ones to apply pressure.

"Are you ladies coming? I'm starving," Vivien said as she came from the direction of Lorna's apartment. Her eyes went to the bloody napkins. "What happened here?"

"There's a first-aid kit in the office," Heather said. "Would you mind grabbing it for me?"

"On it." Vivien hurried to retrieve it.

"I'm sorry if I sounded short with you earlier," Heather said as Lorna continued to press napkins against her hand. Lorna was careful not to make contact with the woman's flesh. They didn't need another emotion-exchanging episode right now. "This thing I can do, it's not something I can turn on or off like a switch. Either I see them or I don't, mostly I don't because I don't want to and I ignore them."

"I understand," Lorna answered. "You don't have to explain if you don't want to."

"Spirits aren't like bumping into someone living who you have to acknowledge or step around. Sometimes they're simply impressions, energy left over from some traumatic event—a heavy feeling when you walk into a room, a chill that runs down your spine for no reason. Other times they're aimless loops, repeating the same past event over and over. We call those residual hauntings. And then there are the few who are aware, like Julia. They come and go as they please, or as their energy allows. I'm not sure how that works. When they talk it's like listening to someone shouting under water. It's difficult and it takes a lot of concentration."

Lorna remembered Heather's reaction when Julia had been communicating with her. She had cupped her ears and seemed drained afterward.

"My hand doesn't hurt," Heather said. "If anything it kind of tingles."

Lorna quickly lifted the corner of the napkins to look before pressing down once more. "There's a lot of blood, but it looks like the bleeding is slowing down. That's good."

"Got it!" Vivien returned with the kit and set it on the concession counter. She pulled out a small antiseptic wipe and tore open the package. "Here."

Heather used it to swipe her palm. She frowned, scrubbing harder.

"Easy," Lorna warned. "It might start bleeding again."

Heather held up her bloody hand. "I don't think so."

Vivien leaned close to look. "I don't see anything."

"That's because it's gone," Heather said.

Lorna frowned. "I saw the cut."

"I *felt* the cut, and yet…" Heather wiggled her fingers. "No cut."

"Then how is there blood?" Vivien asked.

Lorna studied her hand. Weakly, she said, "I think it might have been me. The night I put on the ring I swear my knee was on its way to a deep purple. I could barely walk. Yet, somehow, when I rubbed my hand over it, the bruise and pain went away. Never mind. As I hear myself say it out loud, I know I sound crazy."

"There's one way to find out." Vivien went

behind the counter and took up a knife they used to open packages. She pressed the tip into her thumb and flinched. She held the bleeding digit toward Lorna. "Heal me."

Lorna grabbed a napkin and pressed it over the woman's thumb. "I don't know…"

Heather didn't take her eyes away from Vivien's injury. "Just focus your intentions on Vivien's hand. *Want* to heal her."

Lorna concentrated on the thumb, imagining the puncture wound disappearing as the skin healed. Her hand again tingled with electricity.

"I feel it working," Vivien said.

Lorna pulled the napkin away. Vivien kept her thumb up for inspection.

"You're a finder and a *healer*," Vivien proclaimed.

"I can't believe that worked," Lorna whispered in disbelief. Her hands were shaky. "How did that work?"

"It's us," Vivien said. "I told you. This is our destiny. We're special."

"I feel it too. When we put the rings on…" Heather studied her hand. "Maybe because we were touching each other."

"Something happened when we all touched that book," Lorna added. "It's... It's..."

"Magic," Heather finished when Lorna couldn't think of the right word.

"I can't believe I'm going to say this, but yes. We're magical." Lorna gave a small shake of her head, a little dazed by the reality of what she'd been able to do. "It's the only thing that makes sense. But how? Why us? Why *me*? You both, I understand. You come from families of mediums and psychics. I have never been exceptional at anything. I'm just a nobody."

"Stop that," Vivien scolded. "I can't stand when women our age think they should fade away into the background like life is over. Forget that. I never want to hear you say anything, ever again, that makes it sound like you don't matter. You are special. You are somebody. We all are. We all matter. And I'm clearly not the only one who thinks so. Grandma Julia, from beyond the grave, has brought us together." She paused to fan her face. "And, also, hot flashes can kiss my butt."

"Easy there, menopausal magician." Heather patted Vivien's arm. "Take a deep breath."

"*Peri*-menopausal," Vivien corrected. "And menopause can kiss my butt, too. And ovaries in general. I've been on a period for a freaking month now."

"Okay, I think a certain cranky-pants needs to be fed," Heather said, scooping up her bloody napkins and throwing them away. She quickly disinfected the countertop.

Vivien gave them a sheepish look. "I am a little cranky, aren't I? Sorry about that. My hormones are in overdrive lately."

"I didn't mean to imply that I think I'm worthless," Lorna clarified to Vivien. Her comment had come off negatively, but she hadn't meant it that way. "I'm just saying my female ancestors are housewives, not magical. The only thing noteworthy that happens to the women in my family once they enter their forties is a couple of them got hysterectomies."

"You're not wearing shoes." Vivien looked down at Lorna's feet, abruptly switching the subject. "What were you doing down here without shoes? And who brought the coffee that was upstairs? Is William here?"

"You know he was," Lorna said. "You interrupted us."

"I did what?" Vivien asked. "And what do you mean by interrupt? Interrupt what? Answer the third question first."

"If we're going out in public, I better go up and change." Lorna made a move to leave, not answering Vivien's questions.

Vivien hooked her arm. "Don't you dare. You are perfect the way you are. We'll go through a drive thru. If you don't want to walk on the sidewalk in your socks, I'll carry you to the car. Now, seriously, why and what do you think I interrupted?"

"The clapping," Lorna said.

"What clapping? Heather, do you know what she's talking about?" Vivien asked.

Lorna glanced over her shoulder toward the empty theater. Vivien seemed sincere in her confusion. If the clapping wasn't her, then...? A small shiver worked over her.

"No clue. When I came down they were on the stage looking at the missing hole." Heather moved toward the door and pushed it open. "Wait here. I'll bring my car around."

A streak of white fur shot past them as Ace ran out the front door. The cat made a strange noise.

"I guess his vacation is over," Heather mused, watching him run down the sidewalk in the direction of the bookstore.

"What interruption? What clapping? What

missing hole?" Vivien eyed the two of them. "Will someone please catch me up with what I missed?"

"You do it," Lorna said, slipping out of Vivien's grasp. "I'm going to grab my shoes and find some saline for my dry eyes. I'll be right back down. Don't leave without me."

The last thing she wanted was to be left alone in the haunted theater.

# CHAPTER NINE

The first night alone in her apartment after their failed séance had been rough. Lorna had lain awake, curled under her blanket as she watched each shadow for movement. The problem with ghosts was that they were freaking invisible. So even when they weren't there, it felt like they might be.

Every settling creak and bend of light took on a life of its own. She concentrated so hard that those sounds became possible footsteps and a door opening and closing. Voices from those walking outside appeared to whisper within the room. Even the light from the bathroom didn't help. She contemplated getting a hotel, but that would be a short-term solution to her anxiety, one she couldn't afford more than a few nights. In those lonely hours, it wasn't lost on her that she was a grown woman who needed a night-light and shield of blankets to feel safe.

As it often does, the morning brought clarity to the terrors of night. She was able to laugh at herself for getting little sleep, and for the tired reminder that she had not been courageous, which lingered throughout the rest of the day.

Sounds became nothing more than people moving about in the theater, clapping, laughing, gasping, leaving. Hours blended, as she moved from mindless task to task, stocking and cleaning, locking the doors.

Heather called to check in but didn't stop by, and Lorna could hear the hesitance in her tone. At breakfast, they had all agreed they needed time apart to think clearly about whatever was happening to them. When they were together, inhibitions had dropped and they'd been reckless in their summoning.

During the second night, exhaustion was Lorna's friend, as was the glass of red wine she gulped like medicine to help her sleep. The creaks were there but they weren't as loud as before, their eeriness dulled by sanity. And the shadows remained, crawling over her apartment from the windows, vanquished somewhat by the protective glow coming from the lightbulb in the bathroom. Those footsteps and closing doors that she'd been so sure were real drifted out of her thoughts as dreams rushed in to replace them.

The third night, she forced herself to turn off the bathroom light, as if that act would prove she was the strong, brave, confident woman she believed herself to be. Lorna expected to be haunted by thoughts of ghosts in the darkness, but something unexpected happened instead. She found herself thinking of William and the brief kiss. She couldn't help but wonder what would have happened if they had not been interrupted.

The images that played in her head came like scenes cut from a movie. First he'd smile, the slow, easygoing movement that crept up into his eyes whenever he looked at her. She imagined his hand on her cheek, running down her neck. His fingers would be the perfect combination of rough calluses and gentle caresses. Then she thought of his shirt peeling from his chest, of that strong hand inching up her naked thigh, of his mouth lowering to hers.

Lorna closed her eyes as a shiver of desire worked over her. She brushed her fingers along her naked thigh. It had been a long time since she'd had sex, and even the idea of the imagined touch made her a little hesitant—not because she'd never experienced self-pleasure, but because this was the first time that pleasure came with such a defined face and the memory of a kiss.

William.

Lorna's breath caught. Her limbs stirred under the covers as their lighter weight pressed into her stomach and breasts. The mere thought of him made her heart beat a little faster. Her fingers ventured into her pajama shorts.

*Crick.*

Lorna froze.

*Creeech.*

She pulled her hand out and slowly lifted her head to look toward the direction of the noise. It came from the apartment. Why had she turned the lights off?

Fear caused her breathing to become ragged and she pressed her lips together to try to silence the noise. She waited for what felt like a long time before lowering her head with a small laugh.

"It's an old building," she told herself. "Buildings settle. Heather said she didn't see anything strange here."

With more determination than remaining desire, she tried to pick up where she'd left off as if doing so would prove she wasn't scared.

"William," she whispered, bringing her thoughts back to his mouth. Her fingers slid into her pajama shorts.

*Crick.*

Lorna shot up on the bed. "Who's there?"

No one answered.

She waited. Her eyes moved from shadowed shape to dark corner. Without her contacts, it was difficult to bring objects into focus. She pulled the covers off her legs.

"Go away. You're not welcome here."

A dark flutter moved across the room, so faint her rational mind couldn't be sure it was anything. Yet, considering all that had happened, her rational mind couldn't be trusted.

Lorna quickly moved from the bed, around the partition to the bathroom. She flipped the switch and for a brief second light shone into her apartment from the bathroom door. The bulb popped but, before darkness consumed once more, she saw a figure blocking her way to the stairs. The image was too brief—or perhaps too unhuman—for her to place who it might be.

"Who are you? What do you want?" Lorna yelled, stumbling back as she stared in the direction where she'd seen the figure. She bumped into the stacked washer and dryer unit that took up a corner of her bathroom. She pulled the dryer handle near her head, opening the door but the inside light didn't come on. "You are not welcome here. You need to leave."

She faintly remembered seeing a horror movie where ordering the spirit to leave had worked.

Lorna listened for a response but wasn't sure which would be worse—getting an answer from the undead, or not getting an answer at all.

Lorna wished the lights from Main Street shone brighter into her home. She thought about shutting herself into the bathroom and hiding until daylight. But that would be hours, in the dark, with an unknown spirit that could probably travel through walls so a locked door would do little good.

There was an emergency fire ladder under her bed. She could hook it to a window and climb out to the sidewalk below. No, that would take too long.

She could make a run for the door right past the entity. That seemed like a worse option.

What about her phone? If she could get to it, she could call... Who? Not the police. They'd put her on a psychiatric hold. Heather? Yes, Heather.

Lorna shook as she forced herself to take small steps. Her feet barely lifted from the floor as she shuffled along the partition. The frosted glass felt cold against her hands. Her fingers worked, as she tried to hold on to the smooth surface to keep from falling. She couldn't look away from where the figure had been standing.

She opened her mouth to yet again command the intruder to leave, hoping to scare the spirit away, but the words merely crawled from her throat in a tiny, incoherent grunt.

Lorna wasn't sure how but she made it around the partition to the other side. She hugged close to the wall, picking up her pace as she neared the nightstand. The charger yanked from the phone under her fumbling grasp. The screen lit up, a beacon in the dark. She tapped the screen, turning on the flashlight app.

Light beamed across her apartment. The shadowed figure was gone. She drew the light back and forth, and when she didn't find anything she made a direct path toward the stairs.

One thought filled her mind. Escape.

As she neared the kitchen island, the already chilly temperature in the room dropped to freezing. Her phone flickered and she looked at the screen, watching the full battery icon drain of power until the light shut off.

*Crick.*

"*Lorna.*"

The whisper came from her right. Lorna yelped and ran for the stairs, able to sense more than see where they would be in the dark. She didn't look back as she ran as fast as she could through the theater lobby to the front door.

As her hand pushed the handle, she finally looked behind her. The lobby was empty. Nothing followed her that she could detect.

She felt warmth against her cheek and swiped at the tears that had fallen. The spirit had said her name. It knew her. Could it be their drunken séance worked?

"Glenn?" she asked, not releasing the door. "Is that you? If it's you, please stop scaring me."

The sound of music came softly from beyond the lobby, followed by the static changing of radio station channels. It stopped on a song that had been popular when she first met Glenn.

Emotions rolled through her—fear, amazement, heartache, embarrassment, anger. They became a jumbled mess until she wasn't sure what she was feeling.

"Glenn..."

If he was here...

If this was her chance...

So many times Lorna had thought of all the things she wanted to say to him in a thousand different clever ways. Of course, none of them entered her mind now that she had her chance.

"Why?" she asked, shaking. "How?"

A car drove past, the headlights casting her shadow into the lobby. Lorna let go of the door. The questions brought forth her anger. She wasn't frightened by Glenn in life, and she wasn't going to let him intimidate her in death.

"Damn you, Glenn, twenty years. We were married for twenty years. Three kids. A dozen family vacations. Neighborhood barbeques with Martin's awful potato salad. So, I need to know *why* and *how*." She moved to the center of the lobby, staring into the shadows leading back to her apartment.

The radio turned off.

That was just like him to run away from a confrontation. Any time they argued, he would do anything he could to end it without being on the side of trouble—sweet talk, gifts, distractions of something worse that wasn't his fault. *Nothing* was ever his fault. She'd forgotten how annoying that quality was. It was amazing what someone could learn to put up with in a marriage. Instead of just facing an issue, he'd bury it in anything and everything.

She strode toward the office, pushing thoughts of the paranormal from her mind as she focused on her anger. "Glenn, answer me. I deserve that much."

The radio blipped but didn't play. He was there.

"If you had married her when you were young and then accidentally never finished filing divorce papers, that I could maybe understand, but you had a life with her. Glenn and Cheryl Addams of Norwich, Vermont. You left me to raise our kids every other week while you went to play husband to someone else on your business trips. You let me worry about bills and work as a part-time cashier because we needed the money for Nicholas' asthma treatments, and that was the only place that could give me the hours I needed. All the while you were not only supporting another woman but living in a damned mini-mansion."

Lorna stared into the empty spaces, listening for an answer. If he was still there, the coward didn't make a noise.

"You even used the same wedding ring for both of us," Lorna said in disgust. "Go to hell, you bastard. I want nothing to do with you. I was wrong. You weren't worth summoning for answers. You're a loser, a joke, and a crappy husband!"

Without warning, a cold blast hit her in the chest. It lifted her off the ground and flung her several feet through the air. She landed on her back. The air whooshed from her lungs and she barely had time to process what had happened when her head smacked into the hard floor.

# CHAPTER TEN

"Mrs. Addams? Lorna? Can you hear me, Lorna?" the steady voice came through the darkness of her mind.

"I don't know what happened. I just found her like that," Heather said, sounding farther away. "I didn't try to move her."

"Lorna, can you open your eyes for me?" the voice persisted.

She had the impression of people touching her and wanted to brush off the hands.

"I didn't see anyone else in the theater," William said. "I checked while my sister called 911. It doesn't look like anyone broke in."

"Do you know how she got these bruises on her

chest?" a man asked, his tone different than the first guy.

"No clue," Heather answered. "Do you think she was attacked?"

Someone pried open Lorna's eyelid, simultaneously blinding her with light and awakening her body to the pain radiating through her back and neck. She groaned, trying to turn away.

"There she is," the steady voice said. The man wore a paramedic uniform, but Lorna couldn't focus on his nametag to read it.

"Lorna?" Heather appeared behind the man. "Oh, thank God you're awake."

"Lorna, what happened? Who did this to you?" William came into focus next to his sister. The sight of him caused her thoughts to flash to the night before when she'd imagined him while lying in bed.

She made an incoherent sound in response. Emergency lights from the cars outside created a blinking rhythm on the walls, illuminating their faces through the lobby windows.

"Maybe she tripped," Heather said.

"I'm..." Lorna struggled for the word she wanted as she tried to push the paramedic away. Her thoughts were muddled. "I'm fine. It was a Glenn-demon."

"Who or what is a Glenn-demon?" William asked.

Heather's eyes widened.

"Does she have a history of mental health issues or drug use?" the paramedic asked Heather.

"I don't think so," Heather said.

"Is she on any medications?" the paramedic continued.

"No," Lorna mumbled. She wondered why he wasn't asking her directly. "There isn't any…"

"I'm sorry. I don't know her medical history," Heather stated.

"Heather?" William insisted. "Isn't Glenn the name of her dead husband?"

"She hit her head," Heather dismissed her brother. "She's a little dazed."

"This is what happens when you—" William began.

Heather grabbed her brother's arm and yanked him out of Lorna's eyesight.

Lorna reached to feel her neck, but something blocked her. She tried to sit up, and the paramedic held her down.

"I'll be fine. I felt something and I tripped and…" Lorna tried to reason. Actually, she tried to form a coherent lie.

"Lorna, look at me. Did you say you saw a demon?" the paramedic asked.

"Yes, but I shouldn't tell you that," Lorna thought. At least, she hoped she thought it. The truth would not be her friend in this instance. However, by the concerned look on the man's face maybe she had said it out loud.

"Are you seeing a demon now?" he asked.

"I see..." Lorna tried to look for Heather and William. "I can't move my head. I want to get up."

"That's because we're keeping you stabilized," the paramedic explained. "We want to make sure you didn't hurt your spine. Now I want you to try squeezing my fingers."

"I have to go," Lorna insisted. "You can't keep me if I don't want to be kept."

"What's she saying?" Heather asked. "I can't understand her. Why are her words slurred like that?"

"It looks like you banged your head pretty hard, Lorna," the paramedic said, though by the loud tone of his voice it sounded like he was talking to everyone and not just her. "Try to relax. We're going to take you in and have it looked at by a doctor."

The first thought that popped into Lorna's mind was a protest. Emergency room visits were expensive, as were ambulance rides. She couldn't afford that. Plus, she had to warn Heather that Glenn, or a demon, or something malevolent, was in the theater.

"I can take myself," Lorna said, becoming agitated. "Please let me go."

"We can't let you do that," the paramedic answered. Lorna finally was able to focus on his name.

"Perry, please, I can't afford..." Lorna tried to protest.

"Shh," Heather scolded. "Don't say any more. We'll figure all that out later. Everything is going to be all right."

Lorna remembered yelling at Glenn and feeling a blast of cold flinging her across the room. "I think I fell."

"You did," Heather agreed. "You have a nasty bump on the back of your head."

"You concentrate on doing what the doctors tell you," William added.

The paramedics rolled her to the side and slipped a board underneath her before laying her flat once more.

"Do you want us to call anyone for you?" William asked.

Lorna shook her head as she was lifted onto a gurney for transport.

"Your kids?" Heather offered.

"No. Don't. The twins have classes and Nicholas... No. I don't want to worry them." Lorna stopped protesting about going to the hospital. Being moved jolted her body and caused waves of pain to roll through her. A tear rolled down her temple. Her head throbbed like sharp stabs through her skull. She moaned in protest, trying to lift her hand to her head only to realize she was tied down.

"William, go with her so she's not alone," Heather said. "Lorna, I'm going to finish with the police and then pack a change of clothes for you. Vivien and I will meet you at the hospital. You won't be alone, not even for a second."

As they rolled her outside, Lorna realized she was still in her pajamas but didn't care at the moment. She couldn't see them, but she heard people on the sidewalk and knew she was being watched.

"You can follow us," Perry told William.

"You don't have to." Lorna tried to reach toward William but her arm was pinned.

He took her hand, squeezing lightly. "I'll be right behind you, Lorna. Like Heather said, you won't be left alone. We'll be here to help."

His hand slipped from hers as the paramedics lifted her into the back of their ambulance.

*"...unwitnessed fall..."*

*"...lives alone..."*

"No raccoon eyes or Battle's sign noted upon assessment," a woman stated.

Lorna opened her eyes to find she was surrounded by curtains and the steady beeping of a monitor. What happened to the ambulance?

"It wasn't a raccoon," Lorna tried to explain. A nurse leaned over her and she felt someone holding her hand. "I was attacked by my husband."

"Your husband did this to you?" The nurse had kind eyes. "Do you know where your husband is now?"

"Dead," Lorna murmured, closing her eyes. The throbbing in her head was unbearable.

"Was there another body at the scene?" someone asked, sounding like they stood in another room.

"No. She was alone at the theater downtown," another voice answered. "The EMT reported she claimed she was attacked by invisible demons and became agitated on the ride over."

"Lorna, have you taken anything?" someone asked. "It's okay if you have, but we need to know."

Lorna groaned. The pain quickly went from unbearable to excruciating.

"Get that blood over to the lab," a man ordered. "We'll know if she's on something soon enough."

"He's a ghost," Lorna tried to explain, unable to reopen her eyes. "We should never have brought him back from the grave."

"X-ray is clear. Let's get her up to CT."

Lorna felt her body moving.

"Please, ask Heather. She'll know about the demon," Lorna insisted. "She'll know."

*She'll know...*

She felt someone brushing back her hair.

"Lorna, I'm sorry if Heather scared you with the family ghost stories." William's voice sounded garbled in the darkness.

*Beings tethered to this plane, full of rage...*

*"...swelling doesn't go down with elevation, rest, and medication, we'll have to discuss surgical options..."*

*"...needs to stay for observation..."*

*Come back from the grave...*

"Maybe downtown is being haunted by a demon." Someone gave a small laugh. "Geraldine McKinney came in last week claiming her knee just suddenly bruised as she was walking down a sidewalk on Main Street. It looked like someone—*hey, hand me that IV bag, would you?*—like someone had hit it with a hammer or something but she swears she didn't bump into anything. Then Paul Ambrosio came in for stitches on his hand. He told the charge nurse it just opened up, like someone took an invisible knife to it."

Lorna tried to speak, but a woman shushed her and urged her to rest. Since concentrating was difficult, she took the woman's advice.

*We open the door between two worlds...*

"I have to tell you, you've looked better." Vivien's worried tone belied her teasing words. Lorna wasn't sure if it was a dream or not. "But don't you worry. You'll be out of here soon enough."

"Can you open your eyes for me?"

Lorna obeyed the gentle request. The room sounded quieter than before and people no longer moved around her. Instead of curtains, walls surrounded her. She was alone with the nurse who had kind eyes. "I know you."

The nurse smiled. "You're sounding much better. How are you feeling?"

"Confused." Lorna looked around. Everything kept changing. Whenever she opened her eyes a different person was there. "Where am I?"

"You're at Freewild Cove Hospital. My name is Martha. Do you remember what happened?"

"You have kind eyes, Martha." Lorna shook her head and closed her eyes. "I'm exhausted. Can we talk about this later?"

*We call you to face all you fear. We call you to your eternal hell. Pay the price with this final knell.*

# CHAPTER ELEVEN

COME BACK *from the grave and tell me why.*

Lorna gave a small gasp as she came from the darkness of dreams. It took her a moment to realize she was in a hospital bed. The lights were off and the room dim. She wasn't sure if the dull ache in her head was from her injury or the flood of medicine the hospital had been administering.

She expected a nurse to be in front of her, as there had been one asking her questions and testing her mental state almost every time she'd opened her eyes.

Lorna wasn't sure how long she'd been in the hospital, as pieces came to her in fragments. The doctors were worried about swelling and bleeding in her brain and had her under observation. At first, they weren't giving her anything to help with her headaches until they ruled out certain things, and then they were giving her medication because those things had been ruled out. Someone had mentioned drilling a small hole into her skull and...

Lorna inhaled sharply, instantly reaching to feel around her head for bandages. A weight slipped from her grasp and she turned to see William sitting next to her bed. His head laid on his arm and his hand rested on the covers near where hers had been. Heather slept in a chair, her arms crossed over her chest and her head tilted at what had to be an uncomfortable angle. Vivien had faced a couple of chairs toward each other and was curled up on the small makeshift bed.

Lorna bit her lip as a rush of emotion filled her. Everyone from her old life had stopped checking on her—except for her children. Yet these three who had only known her for a short time were sleeping in her hospital room in positions that would leave a contortionist sore.

She reached for William who was closest and lightly tapped his hand. His head stirred and she briefly drew her fingers over his hair. He blinked as he looked in her direction, and then over his shoulder at Vivien and his sister.

"You're awake," he whispered, lifting in his chair to move closer to where the bed elevated her head. His eyes searched hers.

"You didn't have to stay," she said, keeping her voice low. "You should wake Vivien and Heather and take them home."

"How are you feeling?" He ignored her request. "You sound much better."

"I'm having a little trouble piecing together what happened." Lorna brushed her hair away from her cheek. IV tubing caught on the blankets and tugged where it was taped to her hand. She automatically adjusted the line.

"Heather and I found you on the lobby floor. We were coming in early to check the stage to make sure it was still sturdy. The way you were sprawled out on the floor made it look as if you'd been attacked. The doctor said you had bruises on your chest as if someone had pushed you but we couldn't find evidence of a break in and the doors were locked, though that means very little with those front push handles." He kept his voice low. "I have a new security system being put in tomorrow. The current cameras are too outdated. Heather told the police that they didn't even catch what happened to you. Did someone hide in the theater until after closing?

Did you let someone in? What were you doing downstairs? Do you know how you fell?"

Lorna thought of the cold force striking her and flinging her back. She pressed her hand to her chest. Her bruised skin felt tender. "Something spooked me."

"Do you know what it was? Who?"

Lorna took a deep breath.

"Please don't tell me you still think it was a demon. You told the EMT and the nurses that when they brought you in."

"Did I?" Lorna vaguely recalled rambling something along those lines, but it was all a blur.

"They said confusion is normal with head injuries." He reached to take her hand in his. The warmth of his palm spread over her fingers. She remembered what she'd been doing when the intruding entity had interrupted her. The directness of his gaze appeared so earnest, so concerned.

"I'm not sure what it was." That was about as much truth as she could tell him. "Did they say how long I have to stay here?"

"That depends on how your neuro checks go, but they said possibly tomorrow. The doctor said you're fortunate. With the signs you were showing when you first arrived, they thought you were going to need surgery. Had we not found you when we did... If a few more hours had passed..." He squeezed her hand. "I believe the word miracle was bandied around a few times."

"Bandied?" She gave a small laugh. "Good word."

His lip curled up at the side in the adorable way she liked. "I'm trying to impress you. It is Thursday night after all. I'm trying not to take it personally that you went to all this trouble to avoid going to a restaurant with me."

Thursday? Their date night?

"What happened to Wednesday?" She rubbed her temple.

"You slept through it. This is your second night here," he answered.

"I have to confess," Lorna whispered, glancing around, "as far as dates go, this one isn't making the top ten list." She lifted her arm to show where the IV was taped to her hand. "The wine selection is bland and you brought two chaperones."

William's smile widened. "You're right. I'm sorry. I can do better. You even wore a new gown."

Lorna gave a surprised snort of laughter as she glanced down to the hospital gown she wore. The floral print was faded. She wasn't the first patient to wear it.

Vivien stirred at the sound. She yawned as her eyes met Lorna's. Instantly, she pushed up from her chair bed and reached to give Heather a small shake. "She's up."

"Hmm?" Heather mumbled as she slowly blinked open her eyes. Her gaze found Lorna's and she pushed out of her chair. "You're awake."

The movement must have jarred a sore back because Heather gave a small groan and clutched her side. She lifted her arms over her head slowly, stretching her muscles.

"You didn't have to stay," Lorna said, "but I'm grateful you're here."

"Like we'd leave you alone after what happened," Vivien said from the foot of her bed.

"Lorna, I'm so sorry." Heather came around the side to stand opposite of her brother beside Lorna. "I would never have let you stay in the apartment alone if I thought something was there with you."

"Heather, don't," William scolded. "It wasn't a demon. Encouragement like that isn't helpful."

"Show them," Vivien said.

Lorna leaned forward to sit up straighter. "Show us what?"

Heather glanced around and then pointed toward the chair where she'd been sleeping. "Hand me my phone."

Vivien followed her direction, picked the phone off the floor, and handed it over.

Heather tapped the screen a few times before turning the phone to face Lorna and William. The clip was footage of the lobby. It showed Lorna running toward the front doors before stopping and slowly making her way back inside. The screen blipped with interference but came back in time to show Lorna shouting.

"I thought you said the security tapes didn't record," William said.

"Shh, just watch," Vivien instructed.

Lorna watched the small screen as her body lifted from the floor and flew backward seemingly for no reason. She flinched, remembering the coldness that had hit her. For those few seconds, it had crept into her body and felt like death. She landed on her back, bounced once, and then slid a few inches.

"Who was it?" William tried to snatch the phone from his sister. "I didn't see…"

"Keep watching," Heather moved it out of his reach and continued to hold it for them.

It appeared as if she were alone in the lobby.

Lorna watched as her waist rocked to the side only to fall back into place like she'd been nudged with someone's foot. It happened a few times before suddenly her arm flung over her head. It jerked back and forth as if being violently shaken. The motion rocked her body before she was suddenly dragged a few feet. Her arm dropped.

"That's it. You stay like that until we show up in the morning," Heather said. "I couldn't show the police or the doctors what happened. They'd think we were crazy. They'd put us all on a psych hold."

William grabbed the phone from his sister and replayed the video. "That's impossible."

Lorna ignored him. She stretched her shoulder. Now that she thought about it, her muscles were a little tight. She looked at her wrist where someone would have held her to jerk her around like that. The skin was intact and there were no signs that she'd been touched.

"You said some pretty wild things to the nurses," Vivien said. "They can be excused from the thump you took to the back of the head, but maybe tell them you were watching a scary movie about demons—"

"She doesn't have a television," Heather inserted.

"Fine, reading a book about scary demons. Tell them you confused what you were reading with what you were trying to say," Vivien said. "Tell them you know ghosts aren't real."

"They're not," William muttered to himself, as he kept replaying the video, pausing it and zooming in.

"You keep telling yourself that, Willy," Vivien drawled.

"She's right. They're not going to release you if you don't lie," Heather added.

The door to the room cracked opened before someone softly knocked a few times. A nurse poked her head into the room. "Oh, I see everyone is already awake and waiting for me. Time for your four-hourly neurological assessment."

Heather stepped out of the nurse's way. "She sounds much better. No more slurring."

The nurse nodded in Heather's direction. "Good."

William stood and backed away from the bed but kept hold of his sister's phone.

"And no demons." Lorna gave a pained laugh. "They've been telling me I was a little out of it earlier. That's what I get for reading scary books before bedtime."

"One of the day shift nurses thought you might be onto something. Apparently, we've been getting weird accidents coming in from downtown." The nurse sat on the edge of the bed by Lorna and held up her hand. "Any blurred vision, dizziness, nausea, pain?"

Lorna shook her head in denial. "Little bit of a dull ache like when I oversleep."

"How many fingers?"

"Three," Lorna answered.

"Follow my fingers with your eyes." The woman moved her hand back and forth, up and down.

"What do you mean by weird?" Vivien prompted.

"First a banged-up knee but without anything banging into it. Then a cut on the hand, but supposedly nothing cutting it." The nurse patted Lorna's hand. "And according to your charts, you were pushed but no one was there to do the pushing. Is that what happened? I want you to know you're safe. If you were attacked, you need to tell us."

"No, I wasn't attacked," Lorna said.

"Have you lost consciousness before this?" the nurse asked.

"Only once." Lorna met the nurse's gaze. "At my husband's funeral three years ago. The doctors said it was anxiety induced from the stress. They checked my heart and said it was good." She forced a nervous, dismissive laugh. "This was a stupid accident. I startled myself and then tripped. It's more embarrassing than anything."

"I can give you a little something for the headache if you like," the nurse offered. "It might help you rest."

Lorna shook her head in denial. "I think I'd rather be clearheaded right now."

The nurse nodded in understanding. "Everything is looking very good considering where you were yesterday. The doctor will be around in the morning to do her assessment. But the fact that you no longer see evil spirits will go a long way to getting you out of here. I also noticed the intake paperwork we have on you says you live alone. If they release you, they'll want to know you will have someone around to keep an eye on you. So if there are arrangements you need to make, you should think about it."

"She's coming home with me," Vivien stated. "I have a guest room. She can stay there. I promise we'll keep an eye on her."

"Sounds good. You all try to get some rest. Someone will be back in four hours." The nurse smiled as she grabbed her clipboard. "Use the call button to let us know if we can get you anything, or if you change your mind about that headache medicine."

"I don't suppose you can accidentally delete this hospital bill for me?" Lorna tried to make a joke, even if she was kind of serious. Between the ambulance ride, the medicines, the specialist consultations, CAT scans, x-rays, and whatever else she didn't remember, she didn't even want to think of how much this was going to cost.

"Sorry, I wish I could." The nurse closed the door behind her as she left.

"Technically you were at work. I'll see what the workers' compensation insurance will cover," Heather said. "And I know our health insurance plan isn't the best, but I gave them your card number. We'll figure that out later. I don't want you worrying about it."

It was hard not to. Lorna felt a little teary and rubbed her eyes before they saw.

"And I was serious about you staying with me as my guest," Vivien added, "for as long as you need."

"I would say you don't have to do that," Lorna answered, "but I don't think I can sleep another night alone in that apartment."

"Your legs don't move. There's no way you could have jumped back that far." William still held the phone and had evidently been continually rewatching the video.

"Seriously, William," Vivien muttered. "You're a Warrick. How much evidence do you need?"

Heather placed her hand over the phone to block the video from him. Quietly, she said, "You know. You've always known."

William let his sister take her phone. He looked shaken as he glanced around the room.

"I think I'm going to..." His words trailed off as if he couldn't think of an excuse. "I'm glad you're feeling better, Lorna."

"Thank you for coming," she answered.

He nodded at her, appeared as if he wanted to say more, but then left.

Vivien sighed. "What is it going to take with that man? Grandma Julia coming up to him, holding out her arms and saying, 'Hey, there, grandson, miss me?'"

"He'll get there if he needs to. You didn't grow up in our household with the nagging and anger," Heather said. "Anything supernatural was a punishable offense to my mother. He's spent a lifetime hearing how crazy that side of the family was. Even for Halloween we had to go as something practical—a dentist or nurse or lawyer or garbage man."

With William gone, Lorna felt like she could talk freely. "I thought it was Glenn. Maybe it was. I was in bed, awake, and I started hearing noises in the dark —just weird cricks and creaks. So I went to the bathroom to turn on the light. They flashed on but the bulb instantly went dead. In that second of light, though, I saw a figure in the room. I managed to get to the nightstand and grabbed my phone for a flashlight. The figure was gone but as I was hurrying to go downstairs, I became cold, the phone battery drained of power and died, and I heard someone whisper my name."

"I swear I didn't see or feel any danger," Heather said. She sat on the end of the bed by Lorna's feet. "I would never have left you alone there if I had."

"We should have insisted you stay with one of us." Vivien took the chair William had left behind. She started to reach for Lorna's hand but pulled back before making contact. "Or we should have stayed with you. This wouldn't have happened if we'd been together."

"You don't know that. We could have all ended up in matching gowns," Lorna countered. "We all agreed that we needed to separate to clear our heads. I'm as much to blame as anyone in this situation. I'm a grown woman with three kids. No part of me wanted to think I needed another person to stay with me for protection. Half my marriage I slept alone while Glenn was away. I'm not normally scared of being alone, or the dark, or the sound of an old building settling."

"So, after that what happened?" Heather prompted.

"I made it to the lobby doors. I almost ran outside in my pajama shorts, but then it occurred to me that it wouldn't be ideal to be locked out of my home with a dead cell phone in the middle of the night on Main Street. Plus, I just got pissed off that he was trying to scare me out of my own home. So, as you saw, I yelled at Glenn demanding answers. The radio in the office started playing some song that came out around the time we began dating. I thought he was trying to mollify me. It only made me angrier. I went to confront him, and I guess he didn't like that much. He never was one for taking criticism."

"Had he ever hit you before?" Vivien asked.

Lorna shook her head. "He was more of a people pleaser. He wouldn't have dared. His deal was more guilt trips and subtle digs to make me feel bad about myself. Like the time he bought me an exercise bike for Christmas after the twins were born when I didn't ask for one. Or he would make snide comments. Or come up with any excuse he could think of to disappear from the conversation."

"Jerk," Vivien swore under her breath. "I hate passive aggressive people who do shit like that."

"It might have been the only way he could communicate to get you to be quiet," Heather explained. "If he didn't like being criticized and yelled at, the confrontational approach you took could have set him off. If he was yelling back, or talking, or trying to placate you and you couldn't hear him... I don't know. He might have been confused and not in control of his supernatural strength. If it was him."

"Who else would it be?" Vivien leaned back in the chair and lifted her arms over her head to stretch. "Sam wouldn't have attacked her. He'd have no reason to."

"Have you felt Sam?" Lorna asked.

Vivien dropped her arms and shook her head in denial. "No."

"I'm not a professional ghost hunter, but I've had enough conversations with them to know the confrontational approach of yelling and threats normally isn't advised unless you understand what you're doing and never when you are alone. Normally, questions are asked in a calm tone with a recorder and they play back the answers later. Or they use special scanners that flick through radio stations to pick up signals the spirits can use to choose words and form sentences. I never, personally, needed the tape recorder or scanner so I never tried but that's how they do it."

"So you think Glenn was trying to answer me and I just couldn't hear him? Then he overcompensated with that rush of cold air and knocked me down." Lorna felt a little bit better about that explanation. It beat being attacked by a demon any day. The motions that happened after she fell could have been his attempts to wake her up.

"Intentional or not," Vivien stated with a firm stare, "he could have killed you."

"She's right," Heather agreed. "When you first came in here, they were sure they were going to have to take you up to surgery. If William hadn't agreed to help me check the stage, you might not have been found for hours. They said you would have died if left untreated."

"I guess becoming a ghost myself is one way to make Glenn face me and give me answers," Lorna muttered wryly.

"Not funny." Vivien furrowed her brow. "No dying jokes allowed."

"Your self-healing mojo must have kicked in, thank goodness, because about an hour before you were scheduled to go into surgery, the swelling started to improve," Heather said.

"Oh, and if they ask, I told them Heather had your health proxy. You seemed adamant you didn't want us calling your kids, and everyone in town loves her," Vivien said. "That's how we were able to stay with you and talk to the doctors."

"Yeah, of course, thank you." Lorna nodded. "I'm grateful you were both here. I love my children, but they're not exactly who I'd call in an emergency."

"That reminds me." Heather dug into her pant pocket. She pulled out Lorna's ring. She set it on the bed. "They gave me this to hold for you."

Lorna slipped the ring back onto her forefinger. She'd not realized it was gone before then, but as it settled into place a shiver of electrical current work through her body and she felt better.

"How is your head now?" Vivien asked.

"Little achy, but barely worth mentioning." Lorna ran her fingers over her scalp, searching for lesions or bumps. "I'm more concerned about what that nurse mentioned about the mysterious injuries. I swear I heard people talking about it when I was coming in and out of consciousness. I don't think I'm a healer. I think I accidentally transferred the injuries to someone else. So if I self-healed, does that mean another person has my intracranial swelling and might die?"

Vivien and Heather shared a look.

"What?" Lorna carefully watched their expressions. "Tell me."

"When we went to look for coffee in the cafeteria downstairs, you were still pretty out of it. We heard several people complaining about headaches they couldn't shake," Vivien said. "It was supposed that a flu virus was going around the hospital."

"The only reason we noted it was because we had headaches too but decided none of us knew what head pain was compared to what you were going through," Heather added. "So maybe you did heal yourself, but you spread it around this time."

"You think I crowdsourced an injury?" Lorna frowned.

"I'll ask the nurses in the morning," Vivien said. "I'll see if anyone else has come in with similar injuries."

"Please do." Lorna didn't want her brain to swell up again, but that didn't mean someone else should suffer in her place. She glanced at the door. "Do you think William is all right? Should we call him to check? He seemed pretty upset."

"I'll text him," Heather said. "He won't answer me right away. He'll want time to think. It's best we just give him space to do that."

"You should try to sleep." Vivien pulled the covers up on the bed to lightly tuck Lorna in. "Hopefully the doctor will let you out of here tomorrow. You can come home with me and when you're up for it, we'll go back to the theater and get whatever you need."

CHAPTER TWELVE

Vivien's home was not the bohemian paradise
Lorna expected. Why she thought it would be filled
with lingering hints of patchouli, mismatched
shabby-chic fabrics, and oversized pillows, she wasn't
sure. Instead of matching Vivien's personality, the
home matched the way she dressed—two things that
varied greatly on close reflection.

Like her clothes, the walls of Vivien's home were
carefully considered and decorated. Art prints were
spaced as if measured into place. Though there were
paintings of women, stretched into alluring Renais-
sance poses, they were merely decorative like the
displays of a museum. There were no photographs or
personal tokens, no peeks into the human soul. Vases

stood empty, beautiful and of the perfect height and color to match their surroundings.

This was not a home that looked like people lived there. It was a magazine ad awaiting its inky two-page spread. If emotions were felt in this house, they were hidden behind the protective shell of the walls.

"You have a lovely home," Lorna said, standing in the living room beside the cream-colored couches that looked as if they'd never been used. The statement was true. Everything about the home could be classified as lovely.

"I hate it," Vivien said. "I left everything the way it was after my divorce to remind me of how close I was to being trapped in a loveless marriage with a boring cheat of a man, and that no relationship is better than a relationship that includes the life that was lived behind these walls. Plus, I'm too lazy to change it."

"Now that I doubt," Lorna said. In fact, Lorna would go so far as to say the home was a shield to hide behind, like the tailored clothing Vivien wore. "You don't strike me as too lazy for anything."

Vivien chuckled.

"May I ask you something personal?" Lorna's head felt delicate from her ordeal, and she had to be careful not to turn too quickly or she'd get dizzy.

"Always," Vivien said. "I may choose not to answer, but you may ask."

"Your second husband. If you sense things about people...?"

"With all my psychic powers, why didn't I know he was a boring cheat before I agreed to marry him?" Vivien smiled, though it contradicted the sadness in her eyes. "I think it was because I didn't want to see all his flaws, or maybe I didn't care. On some level, I knew I wouldn't lose myself when I was with him. I had that kind of mad, passionate love with Sam. Rex offered support, money, and travel. I offered a decorated home, a pretty face, and company at business dinners. For a time the arrangement worked, and then it didn't. I'm sure I sound like a nut."

"Life is complicated. People are complicated. They never tell you that when you're young and in love, do they?" Lorna rubbed her temple.

"Enough serious talk." Vivien smiled. "You look beat and doctor's orders are to make you rest so you continue to recover. The guest room is this way. Snoop in any drawer you want and raid the kitchen as often as you like."

Lorna followed Vivien down a long hallway. She opened one of the doors and stepped inside.

A king-sized bed dominated the room. The dark

wood headboard stood tall against the wall and matched a shorter footboard. It centered before a flat screen television mounted on the wall.

"Your bathroom is there. Like I said if you need anything feel free to raid the linen closet or the kitchen. My home is your home. If you need it, use it." Vivien glanced over Lorna's gray yoga pants and green V-neck t-shirt. Heather had brought them to the hospital so she could have something to wear home. "I'd offer to let you raid my closet, but that looks comfy."

"You're not giving me the master suite, are you?" Lorna frowned. "I don't want to take your bedroom."

"This is the guest suite. My room is the door across the hallway." Vivien glanced around the room as if she barely recognized it. She crossed to the window and opened the blinds. "We're close to the beach if you want to go for a walk." She closed the blinds, making the room darker for rest. "I haven't had a guest in the house for a long time. It'll be nice to have you here. Heather is coming by in a few hours. If you're up to it, we'll go to the theater together."

Lorna nodded. The prospect of the theater didn't frighten her, at least not as much as it should have considering her injuries. If she could accept her fall was, if not an accident then a byproduct from being too forceful with Glenn, then it was possible she had nothing to fear once they sent him on his way. She had never feared Glenn in life. It seemed strange that she should fear him in his afterlife.

Then again, she'd never suspected he was a consummate liar and bigamist. What other secrets had he hidden?

She studied her hand and thought of her missing wedding ring. If she were honest with herself, the betrayal was only one sliver of her hurt. No part of her wanted that life back, even without the lies. As Glenn's wife, she'd been drifting. She knew that now. Yes, she'd loved him when she married him, but the years had eaten away at that love like the waves of an ocean dragging at the sands of the shore. Each undulation pulled her down until she drowned in the expectations—wife, mother, PTO president, hostess. For that, she could not blame Glenn. It was something she'd done to herself, with each decision, even those made out of and for love. Being a mother would never be a regret, but the act of setting aside herself during the course of motherhood was unfortunate.

Lorna kicked off her sneakers and walked toward the bathroom. She glanced inside the room but did not see any of the details beyond the impression of a large shower and garden tub. She went to the mirror and pulled at the neckline of her shirt. The two misshapen bruises on her chest had discolored to a sickly yellow which meant they were beginning to heal. She didn't touch them or will them to get better, not wanting to pass them on to someone else.

She again focused on her bare ring finger. William had held her hand while she slept in the hospital. He was nothing like Glenn. When William spoke, it didn't feel like he was trying to pull things out of her for himself. If anything, he kept apologizing for the things his sister might have told her. That was until he'd seen the video on Heather's phone. She hadn't seen him since. It was possible that ended all hope of him wanting to date her.

A cold rush of air crawled down her skin, and she automatically glanced up to see if there was an air conditioning vent in the ceiling. Not finding a source, she backed out of the bathroom. Her apartment had been cold when Glenn came to her. Was this a sign that he was back?

"Glenn?" Lorna whispered. "Is that you?"

The cold followed her, wrapping around her like an embrace. Her limbs became heavy and she felt as if she couldn't move. Her feet became frozen to the floor. Silence surrounded her. A fluttering image along the corner of her peripheral vision caught her attention and she turned to the television. The power was off, and it was angled downward so she could see the reflection of the room on the black screen. She watched it intently, looking for movement.

"Glenn?"

Nothing.

"Sam?" Her voice became softer.

Nothing.

"Hello?" The word was barely audible.

Lorna didn't feel like she was alone in the guest room. She held as still as a fixture, waiting, watching. Her eyes began to dry and her vision blurred. She was afraid to blink, afraid she'd miss something important in the reflection.

"Lorna?"

The low sound pulled her from her trance and she spun around in surprise to see William. He looked as if he was ready for work in faded jeans and work boots. His t-shirt boasted some kind of tavern, but the words were faded.

"Did you hear me knock?"

Lorna glanced at the opened door and then back to the television. The light in the room had shifted and the reflection wasn't as prevalent as before. "I…"

"Heather and Vivien are waiting, but I asked to

talk to you alone first." William cleared his throat and shut the door to give them privacy. "They said you're doing better."

How long had she been staring at the television? By the light it seemed like hours had passed.

It took her a moment to process his question. "Yeah, yes, I am, thank you. I have to go back in a few weeks for a checkup, but as long as I don't have any severe headaches, nausea, difficulty concentrating, or demon sightings they said I should be good to go."

"I'm glad to hear it. You'll let me know if you need anything?"

Lorna nodded. "Thank you."

"I need to tell you something," William said, eyeing the floor.

She stepped toward him and the chill in the air began to dissipate as if releasing her. "What?"

"I..." His eyes lifted to hers and he took a deep breath. "I believe you."

She looked behind her at the television, still a little unsure about their surroundings. The room felt as if it was full of people. Her skin tingled.

"I believe you were attacked by something in the theater. I've spent years trying to deny those little flickers in the corner of my vision. I still feel that we shouldn't stir up ghosts and meddle with the dead."

He came closer to her and appeared as if he wanted to touch her. "The living belong with the living. If the only way to find answers is to ask the dead, then maybe those are things we're not meant to know."

A knock sounded on the door. Vivien shouted through the wood, "Heather and I are going down to the theater. Meet you two there. Take your time. Lock up when you go."

"We won't be long," William answered, not taking his eyes from hers.

"Thank you for believing me." Lorna touched the side of his face without realizing she was going to. He'd shaved, but she felt the slightest pull of new growth along his jaw. "I know that must be difficult for you to admit."

"Not as difficult as seeing you in that hospital bed. I wanted it to be a bad guy who attacked you, someone we could catch with the new security system I had installed this morning. But spirits? I don't know how to protect you from something I can't see or fight." William put his hand over hers, holding it against his cheek. The heat from his body was welcome after the cold.

She could tell he was trying, but that he still had doubts. A lifetime of denial would not be easy to overcome.

"I don't need you to protect me, or fight for me, at least not like that," Lorna said. "I appreciate the sentiment, but I don't want a protector. I want a friend."

"I am your friend," he answered.

"I want to show you something." She pulled her hand from his face and laid it against his chest. Julia's ring was where it belonged on her finger. She felt his heart beating in a steady rhythm against her.

Lorna put her free hand into the neckline of her shirt. He glanced at her cleavage and his lips twitched up at the corner.

She centered her palm over one of the healing bruises. It didn't hurt, not really, and as much as she didn't want to pass along her injury to anyone else, it was the only thing she could think to do. Her heart beat against her fingers, the tempo a little off from his. She stared at Julia's ring, willing the bruise to move from her body to his chest.

"What are you doing?" he whispered. "I feel my skin tingling beneath your hand."

Lorna felt it too. Nothing visible happened, no sparks of light or magical glow. It simply looked as if she touched him. The sensation pulled from her chest, down her arm, and into her fingers. It exploded from her palm where they made contact.

"Lorna?" He placed his hand over hers, holding it against him. More than the injury flowed between them. She felt herself connecting with him. The attraction she felt stirred to life. The desire was always there, simmering beneath the surface. His warmth called to a place deep inside as a way to escape the coldness she'd felt moments before.

What was she waiting for? He liked her. She liked him. Lorna had no reason to overthink or be nervous. The fluttering in her stomach made her feel young, but it's not like she was some teenager. She was a grown woman, with feelings, and needs, and experiences.

The sensation lightened and she slipped her hand from beneath his. She pulled her neckline down to show that one of her bruises was missing. "Seeing is believing."

William looked down his shirt. He made an uncertain sound as he crossed toward the bathroom. He pulled his t-shirt over his head. "How?"

"Vivien said I'm a healer," Lorna answered.

William stared into the mirror and poked the discoloration on his chest.

"I'm not sure how, but I know it has something to do with Julia. It started when I put on your grand-mother's ring." Lorna leaned against the doorframe, unable to help staring at his muscular back. The valley of his spine cut through the muscles, leading to broad shoulders and arms that were made to hold.

She gently touched his bicep to turn him. He didn't move. "I can take the bruise back now."

His eyes met hers in the mirror. "It doesn't hurt."

"Do you believe in...?" Lorna's eyes drifted down to the reflection of his bruise.

"Love at first sight?" he asked.

She gave a small laugh. "I was going to say magic."

He dragged her hand from his arm across the center of his chest. The gesture caused her to come closer to his back as she partially hugged him. "With you I believe in both."

His lip twitched up at the side and she wasn't sure if he was teasing or flirting.

"I'm forty-four," Lorna stated.

"Ok...?" He finally turned around to face her. "I'm forty-nine."

"I've had three children," she continued.

"I've had none," he paused and added, "that I know about."

"I exercise, but not enough. I like carbs and wine and pizza. I—"

"Are you saying you want me to take you out for

Italian food?" he asked. "Because if you're asking me on a date, I'm saying yes."

"I'm saying that I'm about to kiss you, and if you find any of those things I mentioned to be unattractive, you better walk out of this room right now." Lorna wasn't sure where she'd gotten the nerve to say as much, but all of it was true. Her body had curves and scars from a life lived. She had never been the type of woman to have one-night stands or many boyfriends, and part of her envied women who were more confident in their sexuality. But she liked William and desired him. Since she had little confidence in her ability to flirt, she might as well try being blunt.

He cupped her face in his hands and angled her mouth toward his. Very softly, he answered, "I find *everything* about you to be *exactly* what I want."

If it was a line, it was a good one.

She *really* hoped it wasn't just a line.

Lorna waited for him to kiss her. A chill brushed up against her back causing her to shiver. It felt like they were being watched but it was impossible to tell if that were true or her imagination. She naturally moved closer to his warmth.

"What are you waiting for?" He glanced at her mouth.

"I can't tell if I'm excited or nervous," she answered, keeping her words as soft as his.

"I'm hoping for excited."

As if by mutual decision, they came together. Another cold draft hit her back when their lips met, but she didn't let that interrupt them—not like last time when the ghostly clap had sounded in the theater.

The kiss deepened and William gave a soft moan of pleasure as he turned her. She leaned against the doorframe. His hands slid along her sides to rest on her hips.

He leaned back so that his lips hovered near hers. "Are you well enough for this? I don't want to go against your doctor's orders."

This had to be a fantasy. It couldn't be real life.

"That's sweet, but I'm all right." Lorna resumed the kiss. Long neglected parts of her body ached for contact. She stroked his back, exploring the texture of his skin, the gentle slope of his muscles.

William's lips moved down her neck and she gasped for air. She felt dizzy. If she passed out, so be it. There was no way in hell that she was going to ask him to stop what he was doing.

His hands moved just as she imagined they would, firm yet gentle, kneading as they ventured beneath the hem of her shirt and up her back. Warm fingers pressed into her as he pulled her closer. The softer material of her yoga pants was no match for denim. The undefined shape of his arousal teased her with the promise of what was to come.

Lorna slid from where her body was trapped against the doorframe and began backing toward the bed. She pulled him with her. Their lips parted and their movements became fevered. William tugged her t-shirt over her head and tossed it aside. Lorna pushed at her pants. His hands went to his jeans, unbuttoning them.

"Do you have...?" Lorna wasn't prepared for safe sex.

William reached behind and pulled out his wallet. He dug inside, taking out a condom. "Don't take this to mean I expected this on our date, just that I was hopeful."

He grinned. His eyes moved over her body. The smile faded and turned into something much more primal.

William kicked off his boots and shoved the jeans from his hips. Fantasizing about a man and seeing him in the flesh were two very different things. If she had thought about this moment beforehand, standing in her bra and panties, in the daylight, in front of

William, she would have been nervous. But how could she be uneasy when the evidence of his desire was so unmistakable?

"Damn, you're beautiful," he whispered, as if to himself more than to her.

Lorna crawled back onto the bed. He came over her, kissing her as he peeled her bra and panties from her body. She wasn't sure if the lightheaded feeling was from her injury or the feel of his mouth. Either way, she wasn't about to stop. Callused hands cupped her breasts, the combination of rough and tender both arousing and frustrating.

Caresses and kisses overwhelmed her senses as he settled between her legs. All thoughts and worries left her. When he entered her, slow and gentle, her starved body couldn't hold back. She thrust up to meet him and touched everywhere she could reach. Her thighs rubbed along his hips. It had been too long since she felt the intimate contact of a man, and never had it been like this. William was tuned into her body's reactions and quickly learned how she needed to be touched.

Time had no meaning when they were locked in such pleasure. His soft moans joined hers. All the worries and doubt and self-consciousness faded away. Her release came hard and fast, shaking her to the core and making it feel as if her bones melted inside her. She breathed deeply and her limbs fell limp at her sides. William moved onto the bed next to her. He cupped her cheek and gave her one, last, perfect kiss before falling onto his back to stare at the ceiling.

"Yes, I definitely find everything about you to be exactly what I want, Lorna." His hand found hers and he lifted her fingers to his mouth to kiss them before holding her hand against his chest.

She wasn't sure what to say to that.

"I don't know what I did to get so lucky," he continued, "but I promise I'm not going to mess this up."

Lorna wondered if there was something more to his comment but was too relaxed to overthink it. "I promise too."

# CHAPTER THIRTEEN

"I CAN'T BELIEVE I told the paramedics about seeing a demon." Lorna stared at the lobby floor where she'd fallen. Since she didn't remember that part all too clearly, Heather had to point the location out to her. "They must have thought I was losing my mind. Well, I guess with the injury that's exactly what they thought."

"If it's any consolation, I think what Glenn did to you was evil," Vivien said. "So it was kind of the truth."

"Better a serial husband than a serial killer," Lorna quipped.

Vivien's mouth opened in surprise before she laughed. "Clever."

The mention of Glenn didn't sting as much as it

once had. Lorna instantly thought of William, not that she needed one man to get over another. It was more about what being with William represented.

William wasn't the reason Glenn's betrayal no longer hurt as much. He was a factor, yes, but not the cause. Heather and Vivien's friendships were also factors. The reason was simple. After all that had happened, her desperate need for answers had led to a severe head injury. But at least it finally appeared to have knocked some sense into her. She might never know why Glenn did what he did, but she could believe that it wasn't her fault.

Lorna imagined the feel of William's touch lingered on her skin. She had let go of her doubts and control, and she'd allowed herself to have fun with him. The locked box that held her emotions in check burst opened, and she realized she didn't need to keep holding on to the past.

Lorna always told herself she wasn't a silly schoolgirl but a grown woman, yet suddenly she found herself feeling giddy. It wasn't just the sex, though that had been phenomenal and she hoped to do it again very soon. It was the emotional release that came with it, an act of freedom and a symbolic ending to her last relationship.

She had given herself permission to move on.

She had stopped letting embarrassment rule her.

She was no longer Glenn's pretend wife.

Life suddenly looked open and her future filled with potential.

She'd set that emotional baggage down and stepped away.

William walked by the lobby doors and gave a small wave. He'd been talking to a man who stopped him on his way to pick up coffees.

Lorna automatically smiled and waved back.

William winked and grinned.

"Ok, what is up with...?" Vivien demanded, seconds before her eyes widened. "Oh my goodness!"

"What?" Heather looked around the lobby in concern. She noticed her brother seconds before he disappeared past the doors.

"Lorna had sex with William," Vivien blurted as she pointed at Lorna's face. "I know that look. I've had that look, well, not with William obviously, but with this sexy thirty-something the other night. Well done, Lorna."

"I'm happy things are going well for you both," Heather said a little more tactfully, "and I never, *ever* want to discuss my brother's sex life again. Ever."

"Do you know who needs a sex life?" Vivien grinned.

Heather arched a brow.

"I keep hoping you'll find a good man," Vivien said to Heather. "Or more to the point a naughty one."

"I think you have enough libido for all of us," Heather teased. "I don't need a man. I don't mind being single. I like not answering to anyone or being emotionally accountable."

"Fair enough." Vivien agreed. "Though, I don't mean falling in love. I just want you to get a little tuning under the hood."

Heather laughed. "You are so... *something.*"

"A great friend?" Vivien offered.

Heather nodded. "Yeah, that."

Lorna stared in the direction of the office. She felt someone watching them but wasn't sure if it was real or her imagination.

"Hey," Heather touched Lorna's arm in concern, "are you worried about being here?"

Even though the touch joined them, Heather didn't pull away. She appeared to be reading Lorna's emotions. In return, Lorna felt her concern.

"I don't think it matters where we go," Lorna said. "I didn't feel a presence in the hospital, but I think the spirit followed me to Vivien's house. I keep getting these cold chills like an icy invisible force is brushing up against me, trying to get my attention."

"I don't see anything," Heather said, letting go of her arm, "but we all know that doesn't mean there isn't someone there. Trust your instincts."

Vivien lifted her hands to test the air next to Lorna. "It's maybe a little cooler..."

"It's not as bad right now." Lorna walked toward the office and pointed. "Before I was hit, he was over there."

"I'm going upstairs to get the book," Vivien said. "If we do a séance, we're going to need it."

"Grab candles and the flashlight," Heather instructed. "This time we're going to be smart about it."

"Ok, Glenn, if you're up there you better not try pushing me down the stairs or anything," Vivien called as she moved toward the apartment. "I'm not as nice as Lorna."

"It's going to be all right," Heather said when they were alone. "We're going to figure this out."

Lorna nodded.

"Grandma, can you help?" Heather turned around in a circle. "It's strange. I haven't seen her anywhere. Normally, I can catch a glimpse."

"Maybe she's in the theater?" Lorna remembered Heather saying hello to Julia in there.

"Yeah, maybe." Heather went to check.

"Glenn, are you here?" Lorna asked when she was alone in the lobby. She wasn't sure what she would say to him if he answered. Why didn't seem as important. Goodbye, maybe? What was done, was done.

"Help." Vivien appeared at the bottom of the stairs with an armful of supplies, including pillows from her bed and couch.

Lorna rushed over to take the pillows from her.

"I thought we could do this on the stage." Vivien readjusted the book and candles in her arms now that her load was lightened. "It seemed fitting since Julia used to do her séances there."

"I don't see her." Heather returned. She glanced at Lorna. "What's with the pillows?"

"So you don't tweak your old lady hips when we sit on the stage," Vivien answered.

"I would take offense to that, but yeah, I'm still sore. I slept on it wrong." Heather took the candles from Vivien to carry.

"Thank you again for staying with me at the hospital," Lorna said. "It means a lot to me. I know those chairs couldn't have been comfortable."

"I didn't mean for that to sound like a complaint," Heather clarified. "I'm not going to lie though, sleeping in a chair is not great for the joints."

Lorna smiled. "Next time the two of you can just curl up on the bed next to me."

"There better not be a next time," Vivien stated. She pushed through the curtains and strode down the aisle. "Come on, ladies, daylight is wasting and I don't want to try this in the middle of the night."

Moments later, Lorna found herself sitting on the stage floor cushioned by a pillow. The position gave them a full view of their surroundings and felt safer than her apartment somehow.

Vivien sat to Lorna's right and Heather to her left. They formed a tight circle around the book, leaving room for candles between them.

"I wish Julia were here to tell us if we're doing this right," Lorna said.

"Me too." Heather glanced around. "The illustration shows us touching the book, but I think we need to hold hands instead. There's power when we're joined. I don't think we should wait for Glenn to get angry again. I think we need to talk to him and send him on his way."

"I agree," Vivien said.

"All right." Lorna nodded. They'd discussed this

plan at length, but it still made her nervous for a variety of reasons.

"Here I wrote down the words for us." Vivien handed them torn scraps of paper. "No drunken bumbling this time."

Vivien pulled a pair of reading glasses from where they were looped onto her neckline and put them on.

"And we're only asking for Glenn," Heather reminded them. "We need to concentrate on one spirit at a time."

Vivien glanced at the empty theater seats and nodded. Lorna could feel her longing to see Sam, but the woman didn't protest.

"How much time do we have?" Lorna asked.

"All day," Heather said. "I canceled a few of the shows while you were in the hospital. We'll reschedule them later. I think this is more important."

Instead of putting her hand on the book like last time, Heather offered her hand to Lorna to take. Lorna slipped her hand into Heather's, feeling the instant connection between them. Vivien grabbed her other hand and they all three joined.

The lights over the stage flickered, a few of them going out. Daylight didn't penetrate the theater but, thankfully, the candles remained lit. She felt a swirling of emotions. Concern came from Heather. It formed a light knot in her stomach. Excitement came from Vivien, causing her heartbeat to quicken. Lorna wondered what they were picking up from her in return.

"Ready?" Vivien prompted.

Like the first time they'd tried the séance, fear left her as power rushed in. Her body tingled. Heather and Vivien's hair lifted from their shoulders.

Lorna looked down at the paper on the floor in front of her, and they all read aloud, "We open the door between two worlds to call forth the spirit of Glenn Addams."

Lorna glanced up as the temperature around them dropped significantly.

"Come back from the grave so that we may hear," they continued. "Come back from the grave and show yourself to us so that all may see. Come back from the grave and answer for what you have done so that you may be—"

The lights flickered once more going out completely and a pair of transparent feet appeared on top of the book illuminated by candlelight. The fearless euphoria left her to be replaced by panic.

"Judged." The last word left Lorna in a whisper.

She jerked her hands from Vivien and Heather, and crab crawled backward to get away. The reaction was automatic. She willed the feet to disappear. The ghost shifted his weight from one foot to the other, not stepping from the book.

Lorna's heart beat hard and fast, and she had a difficult time catching her breath. Her eyes traveled up transparent dress slacks. Candlelight reflected within the ghost's body, giving him an inner glow. The shadows hid the full details of his face, but she instantly knew him.

"Glenn?" she whispered.

He looked at the candles on the floor, jerking his foot as if the flames and the book kept him trapped.

"Holy crap," Vivien whispered, crawling to where Lorna was on the floor. Heather had stood and rushed to their side. She pulled at Lorna's arm to get her to stand. Vivien was slower to rise to her feet.

"It's him," Lorna said. "I..."

"Ask what you need to," Heather whispered. "I don't know how long he will be here."

"Gl-Glenn?" she stammered. "Can you hear me? It's me, Lorna."

His eyes shifted to her and then away. He looked around, not staying focused on any one thing for too long. His translucent body and clothing lacked substance, but his dress shirt and slacks looked like what he usually wore when he was alive, not what he'd been wearing when they buried him.

Since Lorna had released much of her anger, seeing him now just made her sad. She had loved him once, long ago, before life had dampened the flames. There was so much history there, so many memories. If she could let go of the lie, there might be some truth left in that.

"Glenn, how could you lie to your wives?" Vivien asked. The tone of her voice came much more forcefully. She placed her hand on Lorna's shoulder in support.

"Cheryl?" His word was soft and she wasn't sure she heard it. There was a hollowness to his tone as if it came from the other side of a tunnel. Heather had said the dead could be hard to hear and understand.

"Lorna," Lorna stated, irritated that he mentioned the other woman first.

"Lorna," Glenn repeated. "I can't see you."

She inched closer to him, glancing down at the candles and hoping they kept him where he was.

"Why did you hit me?" she asked.

"I have never hit you," he answered. The words sounded clearer than before but were still distorted. "Where are we?"

"Do you know what happened to you?" Lorna asked. "Do you remember the accident? You were jogging and a car hit you."

Glenn's spirit continued to look around as if lost.

"Why didn't you tell me about Cheryl?" Lorna asked.

"You can't know about her," Glenn said. This time his eyes seemed to find her as he looked directly at her. "That life doesn't concern you."

He said it with such exasperation like he expected she should have known the answer.

"But it does concern me. We have kids together," she insisted.

"I support you and my children," Glenn answered. "That's all that matters."

"No, that's not all that mattered." Lorna felt a tear running down her cheek and swiped at it. "How could you lie to us?"

"You have him," Glenn said it almost like an accusation. His tone became increasingly stronger. "I know you've been thinking about him, seeing him."

"After you died," Lorna corrected. "I never cheated. I never betrayed you."

"You shouldn't know about that." He shook his head, staring at her with an increasingly agitated expression. He lifted his hand as if feeling an invisible barrier. He slapped his palm forward a few times. His body became brighter as if his energy built. Is this what happened before he struck her? "Lorna, where are we?"

"He has no explanation," Lorna said with a shake of her head. Glenn's spirit appeared confused. "I don't know why I expected him to have an excuse, but he's just selfish and a coward. What other reason could there be?"

"Lorna?" he asked. "Where—"

"You're dead. That's where you are," Lorna answered. "I'm here to tell you I know about Cheryl. Our kids know. You hurt us and embarrassed us. She took everything. She left me with nothing. You said you would always take care of us. You lied. But the fact is I don't need you to take care of me. I can take care of myself. It's over, Glenn. I'm here to tell you goodbye."

"I'm dead." Glenn sighed and nodded like she'd seen him do a million times before whenever he became resigned to something he didn't want to accept.

"Yes, and I want you to move on." Lorna felt Vivien's hand on her arm.

"I should have been a better man for you," Glenn said softly, his tone weakening and the light from his body fading. "I should have been the man you deserved. I remember the accident. So many things fall away in death. So many things become clear."

"What things?" Lorna couldn't help herself. Part of her still longed for there to be a reason. Glenn stood before her, but he felt like a stranger. As the father of her children, there would always be an emotional tie there, but it wasn't love. Not anymore.

"Tell her the truth," Heather said, her firm voice sounded like a mother directing an insolent child.

Glenn looked toward the floor as if he couldn't meet her gaze. He stood on the book without appearing to put any weight on it. Considering the fact he was transparent, it would have been easy to assume that he couldn't affect the world around him. However, her recent brush with head trauma said otherwise and Lorna had to remind herself that he could be dangerous and not to take anything for granted. They had no way of knowing if the candles would keep him inside.

"I loved you the best I could, but it was not enough, it was not as much as I loved myself." Glenn looked into the theater, averting his gaze from hers. His tone became hard. "I do not want you to be with this new man. I don't want to share you with another man. I do not want him to love you like you deserve. You are my wife. Mine. I will never let you go."

Had he always sounded so possessive? Maybe in marriage she had thought it sweet and loving. Maybe the distance of three years had given her perspective. Maybe death had added more than a trace of bitterness to him.

"William is a thousand times the man you ever were," Lorna answered. "If I want to be with him, I will. But with or without another man in my life, I'm not yours. I'm mine."

Lorna stared at Glenn, unable to look away. The many, many questions she had no longer mattered. They had all came down to, *why?* And the unvarnished truth to that question was both obvious and disappointing. Glenn was a selfish prick whose charisma and charms she'd fallen for when she was young and naive. At twenty, she had not experienced the world and thought she knew more than she had.

Lorna took a deep breath. "I'm done. I have nothing more to say to you."

"Are you sure you don't want to kick him in the balls?" Vivien asked. "I kind of do."

Lorna shook her head. "No. I don't want to give him any more of my time or energy. I'm not angry or hateful. I'm just ready to let go. I want to continue with the next chapter of my life. I don't want to waste another minute on this man."

Vivien picked one of the scraps of paper off the floor.

"Lorna," Glenn said, his eyes boring into her. "You can't leave me."

Lorna grabbed hold of Heather and Vivien's hands. She felt their connection to her. Their care and support flowed through her, giving her strength through their friendship. "Sorry, Glenn. I already have."

Glenn struggled against his magical restraints. He jerked his legs and flung his arms the best he could. Anger distorted his expression.

Vivien lifted the paper before them. It was difficult in the dim light, but they managed to read, "Spirit we release you into the light."

Glenn's mouth opened wide as if he would shout, but no sound came as his form burst into tiny pieces and fell like ash. She watched as he rained down onto the floor and disappeared.

Vivien dropped her arm. The paper fell to the floor by Lorna's feet.

"Goodbye, Glenn," Lorna whispered. She held tight to Heather and Vivien. Relief flooded her. A weight lifted from her chest, and she felt him leaving. It was over.

Lorna took a deep breath, and then another. She lifted her friends' hands to press against her chest.

"He's gone," Heather said, turning to hug Lorna with her free arm.

Vivien did the same. "I feel the ache leaving you. Heather, do you feel it?"

Heather nodded. "You got what you needed, Lorna. Grandma Julia was right. We're here to help each other heal."

"I thought I had a thousand questions, but really all I needed was to say goodbye and let it all go." Lorna released her hold on their hands. "Thank you, both. I would have never had this chance without you."

When their hands pulled away, she felt weaker, as if she'd just finished an intense workout. Whatever they had done took a lot out of them. The lights flickered, coming back on.

"This confirms it. We're magical." Vivien smiled and took off her reading glasses.

"Grandma Julia always said it took psychic energy to summons ghosts," Heather said. "I now understand what she meant by that. I think the three of us together creates enough energy to make things happen. Alone we're special, but together we're stronger."

"Like everything in life," Lorna agreed. "We're stronger with true friends."

Movement caught Lorna's attention and she turned to the rows of seats. William stood in the aisle looking up at them. He appeared as if he wanted to speak but held back.

"How much do you think he saw?" Lorna asked.

"Most of it," Vivien answered. "He's been standing there a while."

"I brought coffee," he said at their attention, but it was evident by the way he stared at the candles he wasn't thinking about beverages.

"William?" Heather asked. "Are you all right?"

William came toward the stage. "So that was Glenn, huh?"

"Yes." Lorna went to meet him by the stairs. She wondered what William was thinking, if he was jealous or upset. "He's gone now. For good."

"I saw." William nodded. He cupped her cheek. "How are you? Are you all right?"

It turned out he was neither of those things. He was concerned about her.

"Honestly, I feel great," Lorna said. "A little

tired, a little hungry, but relieved. Are you all right? I know ghosts aren't your thing."

"That was..." William nodded. "Yeah, I'm all right. Seeing is believing, and well..."

"Look who has finally come around," Vivien said, teasing lightly. "Welcome to our supernatural book club, Willy."

"I hate when you call me that," William said.

"I know. It's why I do it." Vivien laughed. She went to blow out the candles and gathered them with the book. "I think that's enough undead for the time being."

William gently touched Lorna's arm and gestured for her to walk with him. He guided her by the small of her back as she moved down the stairs. "I heard what that spirit, what *Glenn*, said to you. I know it was private, and I shouldn't have eavesdropped on what you were doing, but you didn't deserve that."

"I'm glad you heard what he said," Lorna looped her arm through his. "I don't know where we're heading in this whatever-we-are, but I know that I don't want secrets between us. I'd rather hear a painful truth than to be lied to any day of the week."

"I hope we're going forward, together, in a relationship," he said.

"I hope so too."

His almost sheepish half smile was hard to resist. Everything about William was attractive, a fact that was all the more real now that she knew him intimately. She liked that smile, his sexy eyes, his sultry voice, his smell, his heat, his kiss, his...

She took a deep breath, steadying her runaway libido as a thought whispered through her mind, *My apartment is right upstairs.*

"We became a little distracted earlier, and I'm not sure I apologized for leaving the hospital as abruptly as I did," he continued. "I should have stayed to make sure you were all right."

William lifted the curtain to the lobby aside and let her pass through first. He glanced at the broken hook. "We should take that off of there. Someone might get hurt."

Lorna ignored the hook. She'd make sure to unscrew the broken piece from the wall later.

"You stayed with me through the worst of my injury. You were there when I woke up." Lorna didn't need an apology from him. He had no reason to apologize. "William, I get why you left the hospital. You needed time to think. All of this," she gestured at the lobby and toward the stage, "is a lot to take in. Especially when I consider that you've been trying to get away from it your whole life. I can handle bad days, and bad moods, and differences of opinion, but it's like I said I can't handle any more secrets and lies. So if you need time to think about something, I want you to take it."

William nodded.

"What we—*what your sister, Vivien, and I*—did in there, what happens when we join hands, the feelings that surged..." She felt a little breathless thinking about it. Excitement flowed inside her at the thought. The lingering effects of the séance left her body tired but her mind alive and very awake. "I want that. What we did, what we can do, I want that in my life. I want to feel special. I want to see where this new chapter leads me. I know I was brought to Freewild Cove for a reason. I thought it was to escape, but it was to find who I was meant to be. Now that I found it, I'm not giving it up for you or anyone. I can't compromise what I want for other people anymore. But, saying that, I understand if you can't be around this. I hope you can. I *really* hope you can."

She touched his cheek and gazed into his eyes.

"I want you to be in my life," Lorna said. "I want to see where this relationship leads. But I won't keep what I do a secret. I won't hide myself in a relationship. I won't fade."

"I would never ask you to give up your independence or change who you are." William covered her hand with his. "Your strength and your kindness is the second thing I noticed about you. The first was that you were sexy. What can I say? I'm a guy, and you were wearing that blue sundress and the wind hit you just right." He cleared his throat, glancing toward the curtains as if to make sure the other two weren't standing there listening. "What you can do with ghosts does not change who you are—someone I'm very attracted to, and who I can see spending the rest of my life with."

"Are you..." She took a step back in surprise. "Are you asking me to...?"

William held up his hands. "No, I'm not proposing. Not now. Not here. Not when you could be suffering from post-concussive symptoms. But, maybe, someday, the right way. I like you, Lorna. I would even go so far to say I'm falling in love with you. I think I've been waiting my entire life to meet a woman like you and now that I have, I'm going to do everything I can to keep you in my life. I'm a patient man. I can wait for you to fall in love with me, too."

Lorna smiled. He was so open, so honest. And, amazingly, she felt she could trust him.

"I don't think you'll be waiting too long," Lorna answered.

William's smile widened. "Yeah?"

Lorna nodded. "I'm pretty sure I'm falling in love with you too."

When she had set down the past it had opened her for future possibilities. William was definitely one of those.

His lips met hers and he pulled her close, lifting her slightly off the floor with his embrace. The kiss instantly became passionate, tongues moving against each other. She felt him grinning against her mouth.

William eased his hold but kept her against him. "Does this mean I can finally take you out on a proper date? I believe you said you liked Italian."

"I have wine upstairs in my apartment and we can order a pizza if you're hungry," Lorna said.

He glanced behind him. "Are you sure you want to stay here after what happened?"

"Glenn's gone. I felt him leave. Plus, this sexy guy I know put in a new security system for me." She glanced up, taking note of the newer camera where the older one had been.

"I'll be sure to let Jackson the installer know you think he's sexy," William teased.

Lorna hit his arm. "I wasn't talking about Jackson, though I'm sure he's lovely."

"I'm serious though. Do you feel comfortable living here alone?"

"I was thinking for tonight, at least, I wouldn't be alone." She arched a brow so he'd get her meaning.

"William, I believe you said something about coffee. I am drained." Heather came into the lobby. She smiled when she saw them together.

"Concession." William tilted his head toward the counter.

"You are my favorite brother," Heather said as she picked up her coffee.

"I'm your only brother," he answered.

"Didn't say it was a hard contest," Heather mumbled before sipping.

"In that case, you're my favorite sister," he said.

Heather gave a small laugh. "Fair enough."

"I'm feeling better. I can work if you need me to." Lorna pulled away from William's embrace but stood close to him. "Do you want to reinstate the movie nights you canceled?"

"Are you up to that?" Heather eyed her, doubtful.

Lorna nodded. "You've done so much for me, offering to help with the insurance and workman's comp stuff. I don't want the theater to lose money when I can run a projector and cash register. I need this job and the apartment."

"You have this job and the apartment as long as you want it." Heather glanced upward. "But are you sure you want to stay here? Vivien said you could move in with her if you want. I think she's excited by the idea of having a roommate. I guarantee you she won't charge you rent if that's a concern. She doesn't need the money."

"Glenn's gone so the threat is also gone." Lorna wasn't going to let her ex chase her out of her job and home. "And, even if he wasn't, I don't think it matters. I felt him follow me to Vivien's house."

"Tonight's showing is already canceled." Heather took another drink of coffee. "Thanks for the offer, but I think we'll stay closed tomorrow too. I'd rather you rest and get better than push it too hard and feel crappy longer."

Vivien appeared carrying the book with her hand inside the pages like a bookmark. She set it on the counter and opened it. "There we are."

Lorna and Heather went to read where Vivien pointed.

A new heading was written on a blank page, "*Three Kick-Ass Women Séances.*"

Beneath the heading, Vivien had started a new ledger entry. *"Lorna Addams, no money to contact lying ex Glenn after his spirit attacked her and caused a serious head injury. Spirit deserves a cosmic kick in the balls. We sent him on his way to the afterlife."*

Lorna gave a short laugh. "Three Kick-Ass Women Séances? It sounds like we need business cards."

"I want t-shirts," Vivien stated.

"I know you're joking, but I don't need another business to run." Heather shook her head. "For the record."

"Doesn't it make you wish we were back in Julia's day—bootlegging, the Spiritualist movement, flapper dresses, roadsters?" Vivien grinned. "We'd be female Capones."

"I think we have about all the excitement we can handle." Heather closed the book.

"I have to pass, too. I'd make a horrible outlaw." Lorna grabbed a coffee cup from the holder.

"Can we at least have a flapper-themed party and wear the fringy dresses? I have a birthday coming up." Vivien opened the book toward the back. She flipped through several pages before stopping at the wine-stained page of séances.

"This was Grandma's book?" William joined

them by the counter. Vivien slid it toward him so he could look at it. His brow furrowed as he turned the pages.

"I'm hungry after that séance. Are you two hungry?" Heather touched her stomach. "I'm craving a German chocolate cake."

"I could definitely go for some sugar," Vivien agreed. "Though why you would want to put coconut on a perfectly good cake is beyond me. Let's make it a black forest cake, chocolate and cherries. Oh, and red velvet."

"I could go for pizza." William glanced up from the pages and winked at Lorna. She couldn't help but smile at the flirtation, relieved that the book didn't appear to bother him. He might be uncomfortable with the afterlife, but he was trying.

"I think that's a hint that they want some alone time," Heather said.

"Getting pizza? Is that what the kids are calling *it* these days?" Vivien smirked. "All right. Come on, Heather. I'll buy you a cupcake."

"I want a whole cake, not a mini cake," Heather corrected.

Vivien hooked Heather by the arm and pulled her toward the front doors.

Lorna watched them walk outside and bit her lip.

"You want to go for cupcakes, too, don't you?" William asked with a chuckle.

Lorna nodded. "Yeah, I feel like I need sugar. Is that all right if we postpone a few hours? I know I said pizza, but..."

"Tonight. Here. Six o'clock. I'll bring the pepperoni," William said.

Lorna grinned. "And cheesy breadsticks."

"All right." He nodded.

"Barbeque chicken wings," she added.

"Whatever you want." William gave her a quick kiss.

"You're amazing." Lorna watched him as she backed toward the front doors, leaving him with Julia's book. "Want me to bring you anything from the bakery for later?"

"Surprise me." He gestured toward the door. "And you better hurry, or they will leave without you."

CHAPTER FOURTEEN

Lorna awoke, sitting up in bed. Soft lights came from outside, moving across the room as a car passed on Main Street. She heard the purr of a loud motor muffled by the walls before silence surrounded her once more.

No, not silence. Breathing.

She looked next to her and smiled into the darkness. William had stayed with her, insisting it was the doctor's orders that she not be left alone. The covers were up to his stomach, but she knew he was naked underneath—and what a beautiful naked he was too.

Lorna slept in her pajama shorts and a cami top, mostly because the room was a little chilly.

It was good to be back in her own space. Vivien had seemed disappointed that her house guest didn't even stay one night. When Lorna had bumped into Vivien's arm, she felt the woman's loneliness. Vivien masked it well, but it was there.

Lorna inched her way off the mattress, careful not to wake William. She reached for her robe hanging over the foot of the bed and threaded it over her arms as she walked toward the stairs. Floorboards creaked gently under her bare feet. She consciously felt for cold drafts. The temperature was warm.

There was a peace to the stillness of night that she'd always enjoyed—those moments when the kids had been in bed and the phone didn't ring. She crept down the stairs. A tiny thread of apprehension threatened, but she pushed through it. Glenn had disappeared like dying embers. She had nothing to fear from him.

Lorna passed the office and headed toward the lobby. Streetlights came through the glass doors. She didn't step too close in case a car came by. The people of Freewild Cove didn't need to see her in her pajamas, at least no more than they already had during her ambulance pick up.

"Not a bad life," she whispered with a smile. "Not bad at—"

Music began to play, softly coming from the direction of the office.

Lorna turned, staring into the shadows. This couldn't be happening. Not again.

"Hello?" she whispered. Her hands trembled and she pressed them together. The music continued.

Lorna touched the back of her head. All outward signs of the trauma were gone, but that didn't mean her brain could take another blow.

"Who's there?" she called louder. "This isn't funny."

"Lorna?" The music abruptly stopped. William came from the darkness. He had pulled on his blue jeans but they were unbuttoned and hung from his hips. His feet were bare. "What are you doing down here?"

"Did you hear that?"

"Hear what?"

"The music." She hurried to his side, not wanting to be alone. "I heard the radio from the office before..."

"I didn't hear music." William brushed her hair back from her face and stared into her eyes. He peered into one, lifting his hand to cast shadow over it, and then did the same to the other. "Your eyes appear to be dilating. Did the doctor say anything about auditory hallucinations?"

"Probably." Lorna gave a short laugh. "After what

we saw, do you think that's what it is? A hallucination?"

"Probably not." He stiffened. "Does this mean Glenn is still here?"

"I don't—"

"Glenn," William shouted angrily. "I want you to listen to me and listen good. I don't care if you are invisible. I will exorcise your ass back into the unknown faster than you can blink. Lorna is with *me* now because she chose to be, and you're going to let her choose what she wants. Do you hear me?"

"William, I don't think you should make him mad," Lorna warned. "Heather said confrontational approaches are bad."

"I'm not going to stand here and let him torment you," William answered. "I—"

*Brrrring.*

Lorna gasped, jumping at the loud sound. It took a moment to register that it was the office phone. She tightly held onto William's arm.

*Brrrring.*

"Do you think that's him?" Lorna whispered. "Can ghosts do that? Heather said that ghost hunters use scanners and that spirits can manipulate the airwaves. It would make sense that they could manipulate phone lines, too."

*Brrrring.*

"There is only one way to find out. Stay here." William held his hand to the side like that would be enough to keep her from following. He strode toward the office. She wasn't sure if it was bravery or bravado that drove his steps.

*Brrrring.*

William slapped the office light on and glanced at her as it revealed she was right behind him. He frowned, clearly not happy she'd followed him.

*Brrrring.*

His hand hesitated and he glanced around the empty office before touching the phone.

*Brrrr—*

William picked up the handset and lifted it to his ear. His eyes met hers and he didn't say anything right away.

"Who is it?" Lorna whispered, holding her breath.

"Hello?" William asked. His eyes widened and he gave a sigh of relief. "Hey, Heather. Why are you calling so late?"

Heather. Lorna let go of her captured breath.

"We must have left our cell phones upstairs," he said. "Sorry. Anyway, what's up?"

His relieved smile faded.

"What is it?" Lorna demanded.

William hit the button for the speakerphone and set the handset down.

"Heather?" Lorna asked. "What's going on?"

"Vivien called me upset," Heather said. "Something's not right."

"Is she hurt?" Lorna's chest instantly became tight. Vivien hadn't been the nicest toward Glenn during the séance. "Did Glenn attack her?"

"No, I..." The phone reception fuzzed and it became difficult to hear what was being said. "Julia... the book... didn't shut..."

"Heather?" William demanded. "Where are you?"

"I'm going to..." The line filled with static.

"Heather?" Lorna shouted toward the phone. The static stopped.

"Heather, are you there?" William asked. "Heather!"

A dark cackle took over the phone call seconds before a click sounded and the line went dead.

"That wasn't Heather's voice at the end," Lorna said. The sinister laugh represented the thing of nightmares.

"I know," William frowned. "Wait by the lobby doors. I'm going upstairs to get my keys. If Vivien called upset, then Heather is probably heading over there."

Lorna was in pajamas and a robe but didn't care. She backed from the office to the lobby. William's footsteps ran up the stairs. "Glenn, if you're there, please don't hurt anyone."

*Thump.*

As if to answer her the sound of a thud came from overhead. She looked up, waiting.

*Thump. Thump-thump-thump-thud.*

The sound skittered before something substantial dropped.

William!

Lorna didn't think as she ran toward the stairs to her apartment. The end of her robe fluttered behind her as she reached the open door. Instantly a cold blast of air passed over her as something rushed at her from above. She stumbled back but managed to keep her footing. She couldn't see her attacker, but that was not surprising.

"William?" she yelled.

Lorna tried again for the stairs. She grabbed ahold of the doorframe to propel her body forward, but suddenly her robe lifted from behind. The material became tight against her arms as she was jerked backward. Her fingers were forced from the door-frame and she flailed.

Lorna landed on her butt and cried out in pain. The robe was pulled from behind and the force of it dragged her several feet across the floor. She thrashed, trying to free herself.

Lorna managed to lift her arms over her head so that the sleeves were tugged off and away. The robe shot into the air only to glide unhampered back down to the floor.

Crying out at the pain radiating from her hip after the landing, she tried crawling toward the stairs. "William!"

Lorna almost made it before her foot was jerked back. Icy fingers wrapped her naked ankle. She screamed as she slid on her stomach, trying to grab hold of the passing floor to stop her progress.

"Glenn, stop," she ordered.

She was flung to the side and rolled a few times until she landed on her back. Luckily her head didn't strike the floor too hard. She tried to push up to look around the empty lobby.

"Show yourself to us so that all may see," Lorna said, praying that part of the séance would work again.

Headlights shone from a passing car, glaring

through the front doors. The light caught in the empty space near her feet to reveal the features of a translucent figure. The flash didn't last long, but the image was unmistakable as it divulged the twisted body of a man with hulking shoulders and muscled arms combined with the large head of a bat. Before the light passed, the creature opened his fanged mouth. Reverberating laughter pierced the silence in hard cracks of sound. In the darkness the creature became invisible once more.

Fear squeezed her chest, cutting off her sound as she gasped for breath.

Not Glenn. Not Glenn.

Demon.

*Demon!*

A scream of terror broke free of her throat. Her legs kicked as she scrambled to escape. Cold swiped her calf as fingers tried to grab hold but she jerked her foot.

Pounding sounded on the door. She caught the image of Heather and Vivien through the glass. Heather fumbled with keys. Lorna tried to push up from the floor to stop them from coming in, but her legs were swiped before she could stand. The air whooshed from her lungs as she landed on her chest.

Heather finally managed to open the door.

"Run," Lorna cried, trying to get them to turn around.

"It's not Glenn," Vivien said.

"Demon—*ahh.*" Lorna was forced across the floor as she was shoved aside. Her limbs shook and she wasn't sure how much more of a beating she could take. Weakly, she tried to order them to leave, "Get out of here."

Heather and Vivien didn't obey. Instead they ran to her. They each took a hand, dragging her with them. She felt their fear through their touch.

"Beings tethered to this plane," Heather and Vivien said in unison while they pulled her with them to the lobby doors, "full of rage and filled with pain. We call you to come near. We call you to face what you fear. We call you to your eternal hell. Pay the price with this final knell."

Vivien slammed her back against the door, causing the small bell overhead to chime.

A loud screech responded to their words. Heather and Vivien knelt next to her side, huddling with her on the floor. The glass pressed into her back. She was too weak to stand.

Flames erupted over the demon's body. It stood in front of the concessions. The screeching became louder and the fiery creature fell onto all fours to charge them. Vivien and Heather screamed as they hugged her from both sides. Lorna felt the heat and braced herself for the end.

The second the flames touched them it dissipated into smoke and ash. Lorna coughed as she inhaled a little. When Heather and Vivien released their hold, gray dust coated the sides of their bodies that had been exposed to the demon.

"We found out what that E-X notation in the book meant," Vivien said, her eyes wide. "Exorcised."

"William," Lorna gasped. "I think he's hurt. Upstairs."

Lorna tried to stand. Vivien held her down, and told Heather, "Go."

Heather didn't answer as she ran toward the office.

Lorna struggled against Vivien's hands, not caring that her body hurt because she needed to see William for herself. "You don't understand. He didn't come downstairs. There is no way he'd hide while I was—"

"Lorna, stop," Vivien commanded. "Heather is checking on him. You're in no condition to help anyone. I need you to tell me what hurts."

*Everything* instantly came to mind. She looked

down at her body to do a mental check of her injuries.

"Is anything broken?" Vivien insisted. "Did you hit your head again?"

Lorna slowly shook her head in denial. "I don't think so. I'm sore and bruised. I landed on my hip pretty hard. What about you? Are you all right? When Heather called..." Lorna flinched and adjusted her weight to take the pressure off her hip.

"Am I...?" Vivien shook her head in disbelief. "I can't believe you're asking about me when your ass is the one that just got kicked by an otherworldly hell spawn. That thing really doesn't like you."

"How did you know what to do?" Lorna again tried to stand and this time Vivien helped her to her feet.

"I was looking through the book and found a tiny entry hidden along the spine of one of the pages." Vivien supported Lorna's arm as they walked toward the stairs. "Long story short, when we tried our drunken séance we messed up by trying to call too many people at once, and not doing it right, and we opened the gateway to let the demon through but didn't close the door all the way afterward. I guess it's a common side effect from summoning a spirit when there is any kind of hostility involved, which is why all those entries have the exorcised notation beside it."

"If the demon followed him, does that mean Glenn is in hell?" Lorna might not love him anymore, but he was the father of her kids. That would always mean something. She tried to pick up her pace to check on William. Though with the way her hip hurt she wasn't sure she could make it up the stairs.

"I don't think that's how it works," Vivien said. "I think we just invited it into our world. Heather was right. We didn't know what we were doing and shouldn't have meddled. I don't think Glenn lied when he said he didn't hit you. That was the demon. But I think it's over."

Movement caught her attention as Heather emerged with William. Blood trickled down the side of his face, but he was awake. His eyes found her and he rushed forward.

"Lorna, what the hell happened? Are you all right?" His hands lifted as if to touch her but he stopped himself. "I'll call an ambulance."

"No," Lorna said. "No more hospital stays. I'll be fine."

"This is not fine," he countered.

"She's a healer," Vivien said. "She'll be all right,

William, don't worry. We'll all share her pain if we need to, but she will be all right."

"Are you...?" Lorna reached to touch the side of her face. Her hand was covered in ash.

"That *thing* knocked me out," William said.

"Demon," Vivien supplied. "It was a demon."

William's eyes narrowed. It understandably did not appear to make him feel better to have a name for his attacker.

"Uh, Viv?" Lorna clutched her side.

"What is it?" Vivien slipped her arm around her back to help support her.

"Any chance that offer to move in is still on the table?" Lorna asked, trying to laugh.

"I'm insisting you do," Vivien said. "I won't take no for an answer this time."

"Thank you because I don't think I can sleep here." Lorna nodded. "And boss, I think I'm going to need that few days off."

Heather gave a short laugh. "You think?"

"Where's your car? Let's get her out of here." William didn't give them time to counter his suggestion. He slipped his arms behind Lorna and lifted her off the floor. He cradled her against his chest. It had been a long time since she'd been carried, but she wasn't about to protest.

Vivien pushed open the door. Heather ran ahead with the keys to unlock her car. Lorna wrapped her arms around William's neck as he carried her from the theater.

"Now, is this all of the rogue spirits and demons, or are there more?" he demanded.

"I think that's it," Vivien said.

"How can you be sure?" William asked.

"Because she's claircognizant," Lorna said.

Heather opened the door to her back seat.

William eased Lorna to the ground and helped her into the car. "I'm not sure I want to ask what you mean by that."

Lorna waited as he ran around to the other side.

Vivien shut Lorna's door before getting into the passenger seat. She turned around to look at Lorna. Heather climbed into the driver's seat.

When William sat next to her, Lorna answered, "It means that Vivien knows things to be real or not without always knowing why. If she says this is it, then I believe her."

Vivien smiled and nodded once before facing forward.

William sat close to her, not putting on his seat belt. "Three days ago I would have disputed that fact, but at this point, I'm just going to go with it."

"Good boy," Vivien said.

"I'll try to drive slow." Heather backed up the car from the parking space.

Lorna closed her eyes. Everything hurt.

"Lorna?" William whispered in concern.

"I'll be all right as soon as I can lay down. It's been a long week."

"You can say that again." William kissed her temple lightly. "Hold on, hon. We'll be there soon."

# CHAPTER FIFTEEN

"Hey beautiful."

Lorna felt the stroke of William's fingers caress her cheek as he whispered against her temple. He'd refused to leave her side as they lay in Vivien's guest room. Lorna was happy for his company. She was especially glad for his help standing in the shower to get the demon ash off.

"Hey handsome," she answered, not opening her eyes.

The bed felt warm and safe. Living with Vivien was not her ideal situation. Lorna liked being on her own, and she was going to miss her apartment, but that seemed like a small tradeoff for being able to rest.

"I have a confession to make," William said.

She peeked at him briefly but decided the room was too bright to open her eyes so she closed them again. "What's that?"

"You know when I said I thought I might be falling in love with you?"

Lorna smiled.

"Now I know I am. When Heather found me and I thought I might have lost you, I don't remember ever being so scared." He kissed her temple.

Lorna finally looked fully at him. His handsome face was close. A bruise had formed along his cheek where he'd been struck.

"I love you, too." Lorna stroked his jaw. The words felt right. "I felt the same way when I heard you being attacked."

"I have another confession." His tone lowered and his eyes filled with promise.

"Oh yeah?" She started to turn only to stop as her sore hip reminded her of why she was on her back.

"You're not the only one in this relationship with magic powers. I'm psychic too."

Lorna leaned her mouth closer to his, wanting his kisses. "I know. You saw ghosts when you were a kid like your sister. Do you see them again?"

He shook his head. "No, my new power is that I can see the future."

"Can you now?" She laughed. "Let me guess, does it involve coffee and donuts?"

"I'm going to ask you to marry me someday, Lorna Addams, and you're going to say yes." He leaned down to kiss her, stopping her from answering.

She chuckled against his mouth. Her sore body made it impossible to do the things she wanted, and she pulled away.

"So was that a hint? Do you want me to get coffee for you?" William asked.

Lorna widened her eyes and pretended to be surprised. "You really are psychic."

"Don't move. I'll be right back." He hopped out of bed and pulled his jeans over his hips.

"I couldn't even if I wanted to," she answered, watching him go.

Alone in the room she kept smiling. Life had a funny way of working out. The attacks had been scary, but somehow the positives outweighed everything else. This was her second chance at living and at love, a new chapter filled with friends and magic. Moving to Freewild Cove was the best decision she'd ever made.

She just hoped there were no more demons.

The End

The Magic Fun Continues!

## Vivien's Story

Order of Magic Book 2: Third Time's a Charm

## Heather's Story

Order of Magic Book 3: The Fourth Power

THIRD TIME'S A CHARM

ORDER OF MAGIC BOOK 2

*Friends don't let friends séance drunk.*

Vivien Stone lost the love of her life over twenty years ago. Now that she's in her forties with a string of meaningless relationships under her belt, she can't help but pine for what might have been. It doesn't help that she's somewhat psychic and can pretty much predict where a relationship is heading before it even starts.

When she and her best friends find a hidden book of séances, Vivien believes it's the perfect opportunity to talk to her lost love. But things don't go as planned and what was meant to be a romantic reunion takes a turn for the bizarre.

Maybe some things (and people) are better left

buried in the past, and what she really needs has been standing in front of her all along.

# THE FOURTH POWER

## ORDER OF MAGIC BOOK 3

Heather Harrison sees ghosts. It's not something she brags about. In fact, she wished she didn't. Communicating (or not communicating) with the dead only leads to heartache, and for her it led to a divorce. For the most part, she's happy being single. She's got a good business, close friends, and a slightly overprotective brother. What more does a forty-something woman need?

When her two best friends beg her for help in contacting loved ones, against her better judgment she can't say no to the séance. But some gateways shouldn't be opened, and some meddling spirits shouldn't be stirred...like that of her Grandma who insists she's "found her a nice man".

The supernaturals have come out to play and it's up to this amateur medium to protect herself and her friends before the danger they summoned comes to bite them in the backside.

# NEWSLETTER

To stay informed about when a new book in the series installments is released, sign up for updates:

Sign up for Michelle's Newsletter

michellepillow.com/author-updates

## ABOUT MICHELLE M. PILLOW

***New York Times* & *USA TODAY***
**Bestselling Author**

Michelle loves to travel and try new things, whether it's a paranormal investigation of an old Vaudeville Theatre or climbing Mayan temples in Belize. She believes life is an adventure fueled by copious amounts of coffee.

Newly relocated to the American South, Michelle is involved in various film and documentary projects with her talented director husband. She is mom to a fantastic artist. And she's managed by a dog and cat who make sure she's meeting her deadlines.

For the most part she can be found wearing pajama pants and working in her office. There may or may not be dancing. It's all part of the creative process.

## Come say hello! Michelle loves talking with readers on social media!

www.MichellePillow.com

facebook.com/AuthorMichellePillow

twitter.com/michellepillow

instagram.com/michellempillow

bookbub.com/authors/michelle-m-pillow

goodreads.com/Michelle_Pillow

amazon.com/author/michellepillow

youtube.com/michellepillow

pinterest.com/michellepillow

LOVE POTIONS

BY MICHELLE M. PILLOW

**Warlocks MacGregor Book 1**

*Contemporary Paranormal Scottish Warlocks*

**2015 Virginia Romance Writers HOLT Medallion Award of Merit recipient for outstanding literary fiction in Paranormal**

*A little magical mischief never hurt anyone until a love potion goes terribly wrong.*

Erik MacGregor is from a line of ancient (and mischievous) Scottish warlocks. He isn't looking for love. After centuries of bachelorhood, it's not even a consideration... until he moves in next door to Lydia Barratt. It's clear the beauty wants nothing to do with him, but he's drawn to her and determined to win her over.

The last thing Lydia needs is an alpha male type meddling in her private life. Just because he's gorgeous, wealthy, and totally rocks a kilt doesn't mean she's going to fall for his seductive charms.

Humans aren't supposed to know about his family's magic or the fact he's a cat shifter. It's better if mortals don't know the paranormal exists. But when a family prank goes terribly wrong, causing Erik to succumb to a love potion, Lydia becomes the target of his sudden and embarrassingly obsessive behavior.

They'll have to find a way to pull Erik out of the spell fast when it becomes clear that Lydia has more than a lovesick warlock to worry about.

## Love Potions Excerpt

*"Ly-di-ah! I sit beneath your window, laaaass, singing 'cause I loooove your a—"*

"For the love of St. Francis of Assisi, someone call a vet. There is an injured animal screaming in pain outside," Charlotte interrupted the flow of music in ill-humor.

Lydia lifted her forehead from the kitchen table. Her windows and doors were all locked, and yet Erik's endlessly verbose singing penetrated the barrier of glass and wood with ease.

Charlotte held her head and blinked heavily. Her red-rimmed eyes were filled with the all too poignant look of a hangover. She took a seat at the table and laid her head down. Her moan sounded something like, "I'm never moving again."

"You need fluids," Lydia prescribed, getting up to pour unsweetened herbal tea from the pitcher in the fridge. She'd mixed it especially for her friend. It was Gramma Annabelle's hangover recipe of willow bark, peppermint, carrot, and ginger. The old lady always had a fresh supply of it in the house while she was alive. Apparently, being a natural witch also meant in partaking in natural liquors. Annabelle had kept a steady supply of moonshine stashed in the basement. If the concert didn't stop soon she might try to find an old bottle.

"*Ly-di-ah!*"

"Omigod. Kill me," Charlotte moaned. "No. Kill him. Then kill me."

"*Ly-di-ah!*"

Erik had been singing for over an hour. At first, he'd tried to come inside. She'd not invited him and the barrier spell sent him sprawling back into the yard. He didn't seem to mind as he found a seat on some landscaping timbers and began his serenade. The last time she'd asked him to be quiet, he'd gotten louder and overly enthusiastic. In fact, she'd been too scared to pull back the curtains for a clearer look, but she was pretty sure he'd been dancing on her lawn, shaking his kilt.

"Omigod," Charlotte muttered, pushing up and angrily going to a window. Then grimacing, she said, "Is he wearing a tux jacket with his kilt?"

"Don't let him see you," Lydia cried out in a panic. It was too late. The song began with renewed force.

"He's..." Charlotte frowned. "I think it's dancing."

Since the damage was done, Lydia joined Charlotte at the window. Erik grinned. He lifted his arms to the side and kicked his legs, bouncing around the yard like a kid on too much sugar. "Maybe it's a traditional Scottish dance?"

Both women tilted their heads in unison as his kilt kicked up to show his perfectly formed ass.

"He's not wearing..." Charlotte began.

"I know. He doesn't," Lydia answered. Damn, the man had a fine body. Too bad Malina's trick had turned him insane.

**To find out more about Michelle's books visit www.MichellePillow.com**